finding home

Other series by
Denise Grover Swank

Mystery:
Rose Gardner Mystery Series
Rose Gardner Investigations
Neely Kate Mystery
Darling Investigations
Carly Moore

Romance:
The Wedding Pact
Bachelor Brotherhood
Off the Subject

Find out more at
denisegroverswank.com

Find out more about
Christine Gael's books
at
christinegael.com

DENISE GROVER SWANK

NEW YORK TIMES BESTSELLING AUTHOR

A N D

CHRISTINE GAEL

finding home

Bluebird
BAY

Chapter One

"Give me a look at that face, you gorgeous girl, you."

Anna Sullivan hunkered deeper into the shallow trench she'd dug, squinting into the viewfinder of her camera. The mother polar bear—named Kona by the small team of biologists Anna shared her lodgings with—turned to face her almost as if on cue as Anna snapped away. In the eleven weeks she'd spent here in Alaska, she'd fallen in love with this place. Especially this time of day. Nautical twilight, it was called. A two-hour window this time of year that lit the sky with celestial hues of deep blue infused with golden starlight... where sunrise and midnight collided.

Only it was eight o'clock in the morning.

As she pulled her face away from the camera, Kona's mouth widened in a yawn that Anna couldn't help but mimic. It was definitely time for some piping hot coffee and a thawing-out session by the wood-burning stove. If she hurried, she might have a shot at getting one of Brynn's famous maple pecan pancakes before the rest of the crew ate them all.

Just as she was about to start packing up her kit, a bleating sound to her right had her pausing to peer through the viewfinder again.

A female muskox plodded through the patchy snow, her calf beside her. As Anna zoomed in, she could make out the knots in the thick, shaggy coat covering her humped back, and the striations of brown and black in her curved horns. Anna snapped away as the calf moved closer to nurse. Not a moment later, the rest of the herd appeared over the northern crest, and Anna watched in wonder as more than two dozen of the creatures surrounded mother and babe.

The massive-looking animals had been indigenous to Alaska but were wiped out by the early nineteen hundreds due to over hunting. It had only been in the last few decades that reintroduction efforts in Alaska had truly begun to pay off, and their numbers had grown to over four thousand. Here in the Arctic National Wildlife Refuge, though, they were a rare sight and one she felt blessed to have captured.

It never got old, she marveled as she studied the herd and then shifted her gaze to the polar bear a hundred yards away.

It was clear by the way the larger animals circled around the females and calves and pawed the ground that they were aware there was a predator in their midst. It was also clear that they were glad to have found some vegetation to feed on that wasn't hidden under a blanket of snow, and a lone bear and her cub weren't going to deter them from gorging.

But Kona wasn't interested in the hairy beasts anyway. She was on the hunt for easier prey like berries, unguarded eggs, or some fish for her and her baby to share.

Anna loved this. She was made for this. Snapping thousands of pictures to capture one single moment that would never be repeated exactly the same way again. She wasn't a crier, but sometimes, her eyes leaked salty water just thinking about how beautiful it was.

Nope. Taking pictures of animals in nature never got old.

Too bad the same couldn't be said for Anna herself…

She set down her camera and blew out a sigh. Then she mentally psyched herself up to stand for a full thirty seconds before she actually made the move to do it.

"Sweet bippy McGhee," she groaned as every ice-cold muscle in her body screamed in protest.

The temperature was about as chilly as she'd expected it to be in Alaska, mid-November. But knowing something and experiencing it were two very different things. And five below zero felt like being encased in ice. If only she could bottle that sensation for those awful, nighttime hot flashes she'd been having the past couple weeks…

Despite her stiffness, she gathered her supplies and packed them up with relative speed, suddenly ravenous.

The trek back to base camp was actually a relief. She'd been lying on her stomach for two hours straight, and she felt instantly better as blood rushed back to her extremities. By the time she reached base camp, she almost felt normal again. With a little food and a hot drink, she'd be ready to get out there for another round.

But for how much longer?

She shoved the maudlin thought away and pushed the door open.

"Hey guys, I'm back," she called, stomping her feet in front of the threshold before stepping inside.

She probably didn't have to announce herself, but two of the young scientists had hit it off, and for the past few weeks now, Anna had suspected that they might be sharing more than just body heat when they went out on their overnight excursions. The last thing she wanted to do was make them uncomfortable by walking in on an intimate moment.

"Just in time! Reece was about to force these last three pancakes down," Brynn said with a chuckle as she stepped into the common room, skillet in hand.

"Save me from myself," Reece groaned, following behind as he rubbed his slightly distended belly. "I ate six already. If I'm not careful, the bears are going to confuse me for a walrus by the time we leave here."

Anna grinned and then bit down on one thick glove to yank it off with her teeth before taking off the other and kicking off her boots.

"I live to serve. Let me at 'em!"

"Steve just put on the percolator, so you'll have a fresh cuppa shortly," Reece said as he made his way toward their shared sleeping quarters. "I've got to get geared up and then head out to take some readings. See you guys at lunchtime."

Brynn shot him a big smile, her gaze lingering on him as he retreated.

"I'm gone in two weeks," Anna said with a wink. "Ivan won't be back until after the holidays, and Steve leaves Sunday. Just going to be the two of you alone up here for a while. If you haven't made a move yet…"

Brynn let out a low laugh, her cheeks going pink as she gestured for Anna to follow her into the kitchen.

"I was sort of waiting for him to make the first move, but so far, he hasn't," the younger woman whispered, craning her neck around Anna to make sure Reece was still out of earshot.

"Waiting doesn't get you a darn thing, unless you work in a restaurant," Anna shot back with a snort, pausing to sniff the air appreciatively. "Those pancakes smell like heaven, but I digress. This isn't the nineteen twenties, Brynn. If you like him, tell him."

Anna pulled her plate and utensil set down from the cupboard and laid it on the table as Brynn set a jug of maple syrup beside them.

"Easy for you to say," Brynn hissed. "You're not the one who has to be stuck alone with him for weeks in a five-hundred-square-foot living space if he rejects me." She forked up the remaining pancakes from the pan and stacked them onto Anna's plate as Anna poured herself a steaming cup of joe.

She took a long pull, burning her mouth and not caring, before she responded. "That's a cop-out. It would be awkward for like two days and you'd be fine. You're both so smart and so evolved, only good can come of it. You're only young once. You'll never be here, in this time of your life, with this person again. Are you going to go back home and kick yourself for not taking a shot at it? Just think about it, that's all I'm saying," Anna added, holding up both hands in surrender. "That's the first and only time I'm going to mention it. I swear on your pancakes."

A grin tugged at Brynn's lips as she set the skillet back on the stove.

"I'll think about it," she agreed and then gestured to Anna's plate. "Now, how are they? I was thinking next time I'll cook them in a little bacon fat to get those edges a little crispier…"

Anna had just finished slathering them with butter and drizzling them with syrup, so she nodded and shoveled a fork-load into her mouth with a purr of sheer joy.

"Magical. Don't change a thing," she said around the bite of food.

She made a mental note to tell Cee-cee about the magic of pecans, maple, and butter together for her cupcake shop creations the next time they spoke.

A stab of unrest poked at her as she took another sip of her coffee. She had spoken to her sister Stephanie last week via the group's shared satellite phone, but her most recent call to Cee-cee had gone unanswered. According to Cee-cee's daughter, Max, she was just really busy with some big holiday baking event and probably hadn't had the chance to get in touch, but it still smarted. After the catastrophic house fire had destroyed their father's house just weeks before Anna had left for Alaska, she had felt much more compelled than usual to check in, and check in often. Despite Stephanie's assurances that Pop was doing fine, aside from driving them all crazy about getting the house rebuilt more quickly than was humanly possible, Anna still couldn't shake that unsettled feeling. Like she'd left the bathwater running or something.

"By the way, fair warning," Brynn was saying as she folded her legs beneath her in a way that only the young and her yoga-loving sister, Stephanie, could manage without dislocating a hip, "Steve said for his hour of show-and-tell tonight, he's going to be introducing us to the all-time greats of smooth jazz."

Anna leaned forward and banged her head against the table softly for dramatic effect.

"Please tell me you're kidding."

"I wish I were," Brynn said with a chuckle.

The nights were long, cold, and boring here at base camp, and a person could only watch so many movies. Their group had instituted Friday Night Show and Tell, where they each got an uninterrupted hour to enlighten the others about something they felt passionate about or wanted to share.

Some weeks were silly, like the time Anna had taught them all how to whistle really loud with their pinkies, or when Ivan had shown them how to play a drinking game called beer pong. Some weeks were sad but eye-opening, like when Brynn had given a heartfelt lecture on the devastating effects of malaria on young children in Third World countries. And still others had been educational, like the time Steve had taught them how to finger knit.

Anna already had a couple of her Christmas presents made, and it wasn't even Thanksgiving yet, which was saying something coming from a last-minute online shopper. She would carry the memories of those evenings with her for years to come.

But she'd leave the smooth jazz.

"It's okay. I've still got that bottle of bourbon socked away," Anna said, waggling her brows as she finished up her pancakes. "We'll hit that right after dinner, and even Kenny G won't bother us."

The two women sat and chatted as Anna drank her coffee. By the time she'd drained her cup, she felt warm, full, and ready for a nap.

Unfortunately, nature was a-calling.

For middle-of-the-night use, they turned to a commode-type contraption they fondly referred to as John. But for daytime, they typically made the sojourn around back to the outhouse.

"I've got to get back to work anyway. This data isn't going to analyze itself," Brynn said as she stood and stretched. "See you later."

Brynn went back into the common room as Anna washed up the remaining dishes. Once she was done, she put her coat and boots back on, slinging her secondary, lightweight digital camera around her neck out of habit, and headed out into the cold.

She'd only gotten halfway to the outhouse when a moving flash of white off to her right caught her eye.

Heart in her throat, she turned and then let out a sigh of relief.

Not a polar bear, but a nimble little arctic fox. It loped through the snow-speckled grass just ten yards away, and she quickened her pace to follow stealthily behind. She lifted the camera and started to snap, grinning as the animal turned to give her a profile shot.

"Show-off," she murmured, moving faster still as the animal padded down a rolling hill toward the tree line. She wasn't wearing her gloves and her bladder was aching, but the fox's shiny black nose and citrine eyes were such a stunning contrast against its pristine coat, she couldn't resist.

Just a few more.

She had just broken into a jog when her foot caught on a loose chunk of ice, and suddenly, she was free-falling. Not one of those graceful tuck-and-rolls they showed in action movies either. This was a full-on, ass-over-teakettle tumble down the icy hill. Instinctively, she pulled her camera close to her body as she rolled. When she finally came to a stop courtesy of a massive tree stump, it was with a dull crunch that made her stomach roil and bile rush to her throat.

For a breathless moment, she lay there, stunned into silence. Adrenaline pounded through her veins, a sweet elixir that let her know she was still alive and which dulled the pain.

But not for long.

When it hit, it was almost blinding and stole the breath from her lungs. She squeezed her eyes closed and tried to counsel herself through it. Pain was just a physiological reaction designed by Mother Nature to keep humans from repeatedly doing something that might damage their hardware.

"Nope, not gonna work," she muttered with a hiss as she tried to sit up and failed.

She didn't need a doctor to tell her she'd broken at least one rib. If that was the extent of the damage, she'd consider herself lucky. With a muttered prayer, she took stock of the rest, gingerly moving each limb, one at a time. Nothing felt great—she'd rolled so many times, every part of her had smacked against the frozen ground more than once—but nothing else felt broken either.

"Okay. That's a good start," she whispered to herself as she wriggled to her side. The motion sent another wave of agony rolling over her and she tried to breathe through it. She couldn't just lie here. She had to get back to base or she was liable to go into true shock and freeze to death before anyone came looking for her. She forced herself to a seated position, using the traitorous tree stump to prop her up—it was the least it could do. Then she tried again to stand.

"Ahhh!" she growled with a mixture of pain, fear, and frustration. Her coat was so bulky and cumbersome, she was already about as limber as a turtle on its back. The rib pain only made it that much more impossible, and if she didn't get to a bathroom soon, she was going to add insult to injury.

It was no use. She had to resort to the nuclear option. The one she'd vowed she would never resort to, whether she was 48 or 98.

"Help!" she called as loudly as she could, dreading the words she had to say next more than she'd ever dreaded anything in the world. "I've fallen, and I can't get up!"

Chapter Two

Stephanie Ketterman stood in front of her stove, stirring a pan of gravy. She couldn't remember the last time her house had been filled with so many people and so much chaos, let alone when she'd made gravy, yet she was loving every single minute of it. She hadn't hosted a family holiday since her beloved husband, Paul, had died in a boating accident two years ago, but over the last few months she'd realized moving forward with her life didn't mean she loved Paul any less. It meant she needed to learn to live a full and happy life without him.

Still, knowing something and following through were two different things, and she was the first to admit her progress had been plenty of two steps forward, one step back. Hosting Thanksgiving for her three kids and her extended family was definitely a step in the right direction, even if she was currently in a state of overwhelm.

Her twenty-four-year-old daughter, Sarah, wrapped an arm around Stephanie's upper back and squeezed. "What can I do to help?"

Stephanie took a quick glance around the bustling kitchen—talk about too many cooks. "I think everything's done." She nodded to her father, who was digging a boney finger into the bowl of cooked dressing to grab a taste. "Let's start herding people out. Start with Pop."

Sarah's eyes flew wide as she lowered her voice to a whisper. "Telling Pop what to do never goes well."

Max, Stephanie's twenty-seven-year-old niece, leaned over the saucepan of green beans she was scooping into a serving bowl. "The trick is to make Pop think it's his idea." She winked. "Watch and learn." She put the now-empty pot in the sink and carried the bowl toward the dining room. "Hey Pop, I think Gabe's drinking your beer."

Max was throwing her brother under the bus, and the grin on her face said she was enjoying every minute of it.

The octogenarian's head popped up. "What?"

"Yeah," Max said as she brushed past him with the green beans. "You might want to check it out."

The older man shuffled at a rapid speed toward the family room, where the sound of a football game was all but drowned out by the sound of men's cheers.

Sarah laughed. "Gotta give it to Max. She definitely knows how to handle him."

Stephanie had been learning how to handle him too. Stephanie's relationship with her father had been uneasy over her fifty years, and it had been tested even more over the past few months since he'd moved in after his house had burned down.

Red Sullivan was a proud man who had never relied on anyone, not even his wife while she'd been living. But his mind had begun to fail him, making him forgetful and, as the summer had progressed, a danger to himself. He'd wandered off, walking down a busy four-lane highway after Anna had hidden his car keys, and even more alarming, he'd used the stove even after Anna had removed the knobs, had forgotten he'd been cooking, and had set the house on fire.

So while the Sullivan family home was being rebuilt, it was agreed that Pop would move into Stephanie's big house. The three bedrooms that had belonged to her kids were unused. Since her younger sister, Anna, was off in Alaska photographing polar bears and her older sister, Celia, had just moved into a second-floor walk-up apartment, that left Stephanie to take him in. She'd hired part-time care workers to help with Pop, but there was no denying that their already-strained relationship was being tested. Or that her father's mental capacity was becoming even more diminished. It was becoming increasingly clear to her that moving Pop back into their rebuilt family home was a disaster in the making. In fact, given his forgetfulness and his increasing belligerence, she was beginning to believe the best place for her father was an assisted living center. If only she could get her sisters on board. They'd had this discussion last summer, but no one had been keen on the idea. She was going to have to bring it up again after Anna came home in a few weeks. Or maybe after the holidays, to avoid stirring the pot during what should be a joyful time of year. Surely she could endure another month?

Right now, she needed to survive Thanksgiving dinner.

She took in the scene before her. Her older sister, Cee-cee, was mashing potatoes, while Stephanie's oldest son, Todd, was carving the turkey, a task that had always been relegated to her husband, Paul, perhaps one of the reasons Stephanie hadn't been able to host a Thanksgiving dinner since his death. Sarah and Gabe's fiancée, Sasha, were helping Max prep veggies. Jeff, Stephanie's youngest child, had just appeared in the kitchen doorway, trying to find a pathway to the refrigerator, likely to get Pop another beer.

Cheers of victory erupted from the living room from Cee-cee's boyfriend Mick, Gabe, and Sarah's boyfriend, Oliver.

In a word? It was a circus.

"Once Todd gets done, I think everything's ready," Max said, reaching for the bowl of dressing on the kitchen island.

Stephanie gave the gravy one last whisk and declared it done. "Then I guess we should start getting everyone to head to the dining room table."

In years past, Paul would have pretended to grumble about being torn away from whatever game was on before planting a big kiss on her lips—in front of the kids and everyone else—declaring loudly that he'd give up everything for just a taste of her Thanksgiving feast. Even a football game. But today the only grumbles coming from the men who had left the game to sit at the table came from Pop over having to walk back and forth so much.

While everyone else got situated in the dining room, Stephanie poured the gravy into a sauce bowl Paul had given her for their first Thanksgiving together. They'd just moved to Minnesota for Stephanie to attend vet school and were hosting a dinner for some of their new friends. She'd expressed her anxiety about not having a proper container for the gravy, and Thanksgiving morning, she'd found the cow-shaped gravy boat on the kitchen counter with a big red bow. But that had been Paul. Always thoughtful. Always worried about her happiness. And now he was gone.

Her thoughts drifted to the mysterious note she'd found in his jacket pocket back in August and she blew out a sigh. Why did that keep popping into her head? Paul had loved her fiercely until the end. He may have made plans to meet someone, but she knew with certainty that he hadn't planned to meet a mistress or to do something nefarious.

She needed to stop thinking about it. There was no way to find out what the note had been about, but more importantly, it didn't matter. They'd had a blissful marriage and nothing would change that.

Tears burned her eyes, and she swiped her cheek with the back of her hand.

"I miss him too," a deep voice said softly from the other side of the island.

Her gaze lifted to her twenty-six-year-old son's dark brown eyes and nodded. Of course he did. Todd had been closer to her but only by a hair. He'd loved and adored his father too.

He laid the carving knife down, pushing a cutting board with the turkey carcass toward the center of the island. "I'm sorry I haven't been home more," he said as he walked around the island toward her. "It's just that it's hard to be here without him."

"I know. I understand." And she did. Some days it was hard for her to be here too.

"But over the past couple of days since I've come back, I realize that it hasn't been fair to you." He swallowed, his eyes shiny with tears. "And it hasn't been fair to me. I've given up time I could be spending with you because I didn't want to face this house without Dad."

Stephanie wrapped her arms around her son, still amazed that the small child who'd loved to spend every moment at her vet clinic had grown up and was nearly a veterinarian himself. "You stop that." Pulling away, she gave him a tight smile. "You're in your last year of vet school. You're too busy to think about me."

"No, Mom. I think about you all the time. I worry about you here all alone, and even more so since Pop has moved in. I know you're putting on a brave front, because that's what you do." Todd grimaced. "God knows I love Pop, but he's one of the most misogynistic men I know. He's never approved of you having a career, let alone owning your own practice. And now he's living with you? That hardly seems fair." He leaned in closer, lowering his voice. "Why doesn't he move in with Aunt Celia? They get along great."

Stephanie looked up at her son in shock. She and her children had never had an outright discussion about her relationship with her father or his thoughts about her, so the fact that Todd had put so much together on his own caught her off guard. She swallowed the lump in her throat, realizing she was in a house surrounded by people, but until this moment, she'd felt utterly alone. Her grief was so isolating, sometimes it felt like she lived on a deserted island in a sea of tears. To know that her son still grieved as deeply as she did made her feel a little less solitary. Still...

"This is a discussion for another time."

"But—"

She reached up on tiptoes to kiss his cheek. "I love you so much for thinking about me, but we'll discuss it later."

"Do you promise to actually discuss it and not sweep it under the rug like you usually do?" he asked.

She smiled. He knew her well. "Yes. I think Max is going to take Pop tomorrow so the four of us can have some time to ourselves."

"Good," Todd said with a dark look in his eyes. "Because frankly, I'm sick of Pop monopolizing every conversation, pretending like he owns the place, and making me feel like I don't belong in our own home." His jaw tensed. "I want our family back, Mom."

She nodded, feeling every word. She knew she should reprimand him for the way he spoke about his grandfather, but he wasn't wrong. Truth be told, Stephanie hadn't felt comfortable in her house for months. "We'll have a family meeting tomorrow." The thought made her stomach knot with anxiety, but he was right. It was a discussion that needed to happen. "But for now, we'll put smiles on our faces and go celebrate Thanksgiving with our family." She paused. "I want you to sit at the head of the table."

His eyes flew wide. "Why?"

"With your father gone..."

"*You* are the head of our family now, Mom, not me." His body stiffened. "If Pop doesn't like it, he can shove it up his—"

"Okay," she said, her stomach plummeting as she realized her son had hit the nail on the head. She'd inadvertently decided to offer the seat to Todd to avoid a confrontation with her father. "You're right."

He grinned. "Just be sure to back me up later when I tell Sarah and Jeff you said that."

She laughed, her heart aching. She'd missed him so much. "Done. And if you need to run away after they try to beat the gloating out of you, you can head over to my office and take a peek at Shelley. He's going to be ready to go soon, and I'm trying to decide whether to keep him at the office until spring or call the aquarium in Portland and see if they can take him." Beckett Wright had come upon the giant turtle while out on a tow truck run and had brought the injured animal to Stephanie's office. The massive turtle had been gravely injured, its shell cracked in two, after having been hit by a car. Stephanie, with the help of Cee-cee's boyfriend Mick, had spent hours patching him back together with wire and shellac. He'd been living in a kiddie pool in her office ever since. "He'd probably be better off with more space and some turtle friends."

His mouth parted. "Sorry, Mom, I know that's going to be tough. You didn't mention that when I was looking him over yesterday."

It hadn't been on her radar yesterday, but talking to her son made her realize that Shelley had been ready to go for weeks. She couldn't release him now—the water temperature would kill him due to a phenomenon called cold stunning—but it was past time for him to go somewhere with room to swim and to reacclimate to life in the water. Stephanie had been clinging to the turtle for personal reasons she wasn't about to explore right now. She had a meal to serve.

"Ready to face the beast?" she teased, picking up the gravy bowl.

Todd lifted the platter of turkey meat. "You're the one who needs to gird her loins."

Laughing, the two of them walked into the dining room to lay the turkey and gravy on the table. Cee-cee, Mick, Gabe, Sasha, and Max sat one side, with Pop at the end. Jeff, Oliver, and Sarah sat on the other, with an empty chair beside them and one facing opposite Pop.

Taking a deep breath, Stephanie sat down at the head of the table while Todd sat to her right.

Pop's brow lowered into a deep scowl. "What are you doing sittin' there?" He gestured to Todd. "Take your place at the head of the table, boy."

Everyone fell silent and tension filled the air.

"Don't be silly, Pop," Cee-cee said with a bright smile. "Of course Stephanie should sit at the head of her own table."

"Todd's the man of the house now," Pop said. "He needs to take his place." He shot his grandson a pointed look. "Why are you still sitting there, boy? Move!"

Everyone stared at the older man in stunned silence, and even Stephanie was in shock. This was a lot coming from him, even if he had been more belligerent lately.

Todd squared his shoulders, and said in a stiff voice, "My mother is the head of our family now, and I'm not sure what it says about you if you haven't recognized that."

"Todd," Stephanie warned under her breath.

Pop shook his head. "The man is supposed to be at the head, and since your father's gone, it's up to you to man up."

Those last two words lit a fire in Stephanie's blood. "Man up? Are you insinuating my son isn't masculine enough? It's the fricking twenty-first century, Pop. You can't say things like that anymore."

Pop's jaw locked. "Well, back in my day—"

"It's not your day anymore, Pop," Todd snapped, anger blazing in his eyes. "And I won't stand for you to belittle my mother in her own house."

"Todd!" Max gasped. She placed a hand on her grandfather's arm. "He's an old man."

Pop shrugged off her hand. "Who are you callin' an old man?"

"Pop," Cee-cee said softly. "Stop. This is Stephanie's house."

"Bullcrap," he snorted. "I live here now, which makes it just as much mine."

Todd's chair shot back as he got to his feet. "Excuse me? How do you figure that?"

Pop shot him a withering glare. "Who do you think paid for that college education her mother insisted on?"

"You think it was an investment?" Todd asked, his face red. *"Like a 401K plan?"*

"Todd," Stephanie said, standing next to her son and tugging on his arm. "Not now. Just let it go."

"Let it go?" Todd demanded, clearly upset. "He's *insulting* you, Mom. How do you expect me to let it go?"

"Kids these days," Pop muttered, reaching for a roll from the basket next to him. "All we need is Anna here to stir the pot even more."

"Ask and you shall receive," a voice said from the living room. Seconds later, Stephanie's sister Anna hobbled into view, clutching her side. Her face was covered in bruises. "Sounds like I'm missing the most exciting Thanksgiving ever!"

Chapter Three

Judging by the stunned looks on the faces of her loved ones, either Anna was looking even rougher than she'd thought, or she'd really done a stellar job of surprising them by crashing this shindig.

And what a shindig it was, apparently. On the way over, she'd been really enjoying the crisp autumn day, the smell of apples and fallen leaves filling the air. It was a welcome change from the frozen tundra she'd left. But not even Alaska felt as icy as the room she'd just stepped into. Luckily, it seemed like her appearance had derailed all that as everyone gaped at her.

Stephanie blinked, wide-eyed and speechless, as Cee-cee's jaw went slack. Cee-cee's daughter, Max, was the first to break the heavy silence as she gasped, pushing her chair to stand.

"Aunt Anna? Oh my God, what's happened to you?"

Cee-cee hopped up next, followed by Steph and then pretty much everyone else. They all rushed to crowd around her with the exception of some kid with a goatee and spiky hair she'd never seen before.

"I'm fine, I'm fine," she assured them with a forced chuckle as they took turns examining her and wincing while they peppered her with questions. "It looks way more serious than it is. The polar bear got the worst of it, for sure."

"Polar bear?" Pop thundered, still ambling over and coming to a stop as his bushy brows caved into a scowl. "See, this is what happens when you go off gallivanting around the world to foreign countries and live like some kinda pirate or something. Why can't you be more like Cee-cee and bake cakes or something women are supposed to do?"

The room broke into a collective groan, which even the goatee kid joined in on, as Anna rolled her eyes at her father.

Note to self: Don't let Pop in on the whole finger-knitting thing. It would give the old man way too much joy.

"First of all, Alaska isn't a foreign country. It's part of the United States, Pop. Second of all, I don't live like a pirate, whatever that means. Third of all, I was just kidding about the polar bear. It was more the fault of an arctic fox, which I will get into once I've had a hot second to take my coat off and get a drink."

Because a big, fat drink was clearly needed if she hoped to get through this day with her sanity intact.

"Everyone sit and start eating before it gets cold while I get Anna's coat and fix her a glass of wine, hmm?" Stephanie said. She took Anna's hand and pulled her away without waiting for a reply.

"Thanks, sis," Anna whispered, letting out the breath she'd been holding as she gingerly shrugged off her coat.

She'd expected chaos. After all, they hadn't expected her home for at least a few more weeks and her physical appearance was definitely a showstopper, but she hadn't expected the instant rush of tension. She was wound up tighter than a German clock right now, and she'd been home less than twenty-four hours. Maybe this had been a mistake. Maybe she should've taken Brynn up on her offer to use her apartment in Colorado for the first few weeks of recovery.

"No, thank you. It was getting ugly in there and your timing was perfect. But that's not important right now. Tell me, what really happened to you?" Stephanie asked as she slung Anna's coat on the bannister as they passed down the hall and into the kitchen. "You can make jokes with the rest of them, but I know how scary whatever it was must've been. Those are some serious contusions, and I'm sure they aren't limited to your face."

Leave it to Dr. Steph to get to the heart of things, stat.

"Actually, the polar bear joke wasn't me trying to downplay the incident." Or, at least it wasn't *just* that. "Fact is that it sounds way less humiliating than the truth," she said as Steph gestured to a seat at the kitchen island and Anna slid carefully onto it.

"And the truth is…?"

"That I had to pee super bad, went outside, got waylaid by a gorgeous arctic fox, slipped and went careening down an icy hill, then used a massive tree stump to break my fall."

Steph flinched in sympathy as she bustled over to the cabinets to get a wine glass. "Ouch. So I'm guessing ribs and what else? Broken or just bruised? Let me see."

Anna hesitated and then lifted the hem of her cable-knit sweater, awaiting her sister's horrified gasp. She looked like someone had painted her skin from the underside of her breast down to her hip bone in a mottled blend of purple and black and used three coats to do it.

"Just the ribs. Fractured a few, yeah. Apparently, they don't have you bind them or anything anymore. They just have to let them heal on their own. And then of course my lovely face," she said, letting her sweater fall back into place as she gestured to the bruises that covered her cheekbone and eye socket. "I didn't pee myself, for what it's worth. But I did have to call out for help. Life Alert style."

"Oh, no, Anna. You didn't...," Steph murmured, slipping the now-full wine glass into Anna's hand.

Her sisters were both well aware of her feelings on invoking the old '80s commercial with an elderly woman helpless at the bottom of the steps. They'd all agreed that it was the ultimate sign of aging, and one she didn't think she'd have to resort to until she was at least eighty. It had been a tough pill to swallow, and one Anna was still coming to terms with on multiple levels. She tried to keep things light and look at the funny side of life, but the feeling of helplessness and fragility had scared her down to the toes of her boots.

"Sorry, I was going to come right in but had to talk Pop out of following me," Cee-cee called breathlessly as she breezed in, rushing to Anna's side. "He won't say it, but he feels bad. I don't think he meant what he said. He was just scared because it looks so bad. Now tell me everything. Wait. No," she corrected, holding up one hand. "Start with telling me you're okay and then go from there."

"I'm fine," Anna said, pausing to take a long pull from her glass before continuing. "Long story short, I had to pee, slid down a hill, and broke a few ribs. Long, rather uncomfortable recovery time, but nothing serious in the scheme of things."

Cee-cee let out a sigh and nodded. "Okay, that's good. I can handle that. I'm obviously not thrilled about the circumstances, but I have to admit, I love having you home for the holidays. We missed you."

Anna's eyes stung, suspiciously close to tearing up, and she blinked hard. "Yeah, I missed you guys too. Although from what I heard when I walked in, seems like things are still peachy keen as ever," she chirped, happy to switch the focus from her injuries and maudlin thoughts about aging. "Pop's in fine form, huh?"

Stephanie groaned and slumped one hip against the island, like someone had sucked the air right out of her. "He's literally killing me. Sarah is willing to roll her eyes and ignore it, and Jeff is sort of clueless most of the time, but Todd has had it with his sexist, backward thinking. Apparently, it reached a boiling point today. Todd felt like I should sit at the head of the table, and Pop disagreed." Steph pursed her lips and grabbed Anna's wine glass and took a sip before handing it back. "He's getting worse. His dementia doesn't seem to be getting worse, exactly. More like being out of his element and having his whole routine shaken up since the fire has made him irritable and more difficult."

Steph and Pop didn't get on especially well on the best of days. If their father was even more of a treat than usual, Anna could only imagine that Steph was ready to leap out the nearest window. She'd sensed the tension in her sister during their last couple phone calls, but she didn't realize things had gotten to this level.

She fought past the prickle of guilt and tried to focus on problem-solving instead. "I can't do a whole lot for him physically right now. I'm not even supposed to be driving, technically. But I'm happy to give you a few hours every other evening and just sit with him so you can get out."

"It's not even that," Steph said with a helpless shrug. "Eva's been a godsend, but she can't be here twenty-four seven. No one can. Despite my being at work a lot of the day, it's a lot. He's got an opinion on everything. I can't make the coffee strong enough one day, and it's too strong the next. He's mad I won't let him cook for himself, he doesn't like how soft the mattress on his bed is. You name it, he's got a complaint. The two of us in one house is just like oil and water."

"A great starter for a salad dressing, but not so hot when it comes to familial relationships," Cee-cee said, shaking her head.

"Which reminds me, Anna, I'm running a pet adoption event at the community center on Sunday. The whole family will be there, if you're feeling up to it and want to stop by?"

Anna nodded, making a mental note to take it easy the night before so she wasn't too sore.. "Sounds good. Wouldn't miss it."

"Everyone okay in here?"

The three sisters turned to find Sarah in the doorway, concern marring her pretty face.

"Absolutely. We'll be out in two shakes, Peanut," Anna said, using the nickname she'd given her niece when she was a toddler.

A bubble of laughter burst from Cee-cee's mouth and Anna turned to find Steph shooting her a death stare as Sarah disappeared back into the dining room.

"What?" Anna said, shrugging. "It's been like twenty-five years, get over it."

"It's just ridiculous, that's all," Steph said, her lips twitching as she fought a smile.

Not having kids of her own, Anna hadn't been hip to all the stuff about raising them. There were rules about everything from hot dogs and sleeping positions to car seats and diaper rash cream. Apparently, even grapes weren't safe! On top of that, she would frequently get her two nieces mixed up when it came to their likes and dislikes and what their mothers permitted them to have when she babysat them. So, when Sarah had been diagnosed with a mild nut allergy, Anna had taken to calling her Peanut... not so much as a term of endearment, but more as a reminder. To Steph's everlasting chagrin, it stuck.

"I'm just glad 'Squirt' didn't stick after that time Max peed the bed," Cee-cee said with a snort.

"If you think about it, Steph, it really is the truest expression of love, seeing as how I did it because I didn't want Sarah to break out in a rash," Anna reasoned, grinning as Cee-cee's chuckles turned to full-blown laughter and Steph's smile finally broke free from the chains of propriety.

"Or you could've, you know, just learned the difference between our kids," Steph said.

"I was young and I had a lot of important things to think about and keep track of back then," Anna retorted with faux indignance.

"You managed to keep track of all your boyfriends just fine," Cee-cee crowed and began ticking them off on her fingers. "Let's see, there was Dave, Andrew, Trey, Patrick—"

"Oooh, Patrick. He was a hunk, wasn't he?" Anna squealed, fanning herself.

As the three of them giggled like teenagers, the tension that had been gripping her like a vice slowly began to unfurl.

This.

This was what she'd missed while she was away. The connection. The knowledge that you were in a place where people knew you and accepted you, warts and all. Not that they didn't fight. Heck, she and Steph especially had butted heads more times over the past six months than she could count. And sure, caring for an elderly parent could be tough sometimes and cause tension. But at the end of the day, her sisters were her anchors. They kept her stable, grounded, and humble.

Anchors also keep things in place, a little voice in her head chimed in.

She shoved the thought aside and focused on the good stuff. The smell of butter-basted turkey lingering in the air, with hints of a baking pumpkin pie in the background. The laughter and camaraderie of her sisters, who also happened to be her best friends. And the fact that she was home in Bluebird Bay for the holidays.

What could be better than that?

"If you three don't get your scrawny butts out here, the food's gonna be gone and I could be dead for all you know!" Pop bellowed from the dining room.

"See?" Cee-cee said with a rueful chuckle. "He loves us and wants to make sure we have food to eat."

"Yeah, he's all heart." Steph shook her head and smoothed a hand over her hair, shooting them both an overly bright smile. "So let's go out there and enjoy some more Sullivan family fun, shall we?"

Anna held up a finger, drained her glass, and tipped it toward Steph for a refill before holding it aloft with a grin.

"To Thanksgiving, where the pearl onions and Jell-O molds aren't the only things that are hard to swallow. And to Pop. May he be less salty than the gravy, for once."

Her sisters held imaginary glasses high and nodded.

"Hear, hear!"

Chapter Four

Celia Burrows was a busy woman. Downtown Bluebird Bay was typically slow in the winter, but the chamber of commerce had decided to try to boost business for the shops and restaurants that remained open all year long. They'd begun having monthly events that brought in tourists not only for the day, but for the weekend. October had featured Halloween the last weekend of the month with trick-or-treating, pumpkin-carving contests, fall floral arranging classes, and of course cupcake decorating at Celia's shop. The weekends had been a smashing success, and the Christmas theme they had arranged for Thanksgiving weekend had—so far—been even better. Now it was four p.m. on Black Friday and she'd sold out of just about everything—and she'd quadrupled her usual number of cupcakes. They'd had their first lull in hours, so she took pity on poor Pete, the high school kid who helped out in the afternoons and on weekends, and told him to cut out early.

"Thanks, Celia," he said with a wide smile. "I definitely won't say no to that!"

She chuckled as he got his stuff together, lickety-split, and took off out the door. Then her thoughts turned to the

East Coast Holiday Cupcake Battle, a huge baking and decorating contest that could put Cee-cee's Cupcake's in the national spotlight. If she had any hope of making it to the finals, let alone winning the $50,000 grand prize, she'd have to give it a lot of time and attention. Time and attention that already seemed to be spread so thin since the move and opening of the shop.

The front door dinged and she was about to let her customer know that the only cupcakes she had left were five cookies and cream and a couple of lavender vanilla, but it was her ex-husband Nate.

Ex-husband.

After thirty years of marriage, Nate had only been her ex-husband for about four months, but it felt like a lifetime. Her life had changed so much since that day she'd come home and found out he'd left her for another woman, their realtor, Amanda Meadows. Celia had lost herself in her marriage, and as soon as she worked through her shock, she embraced her new life with gusto. With her kids grown, Celia decided to focus on herself for once. Now she had a thriving cupcake shop and her sexy, amazingly supportive boyfriend, Mick, and her life was near perfect. Not totally perfect. Her daughter Max's new bookstore wasn't thriving like Cee-cee's Cupcakes, and then there was the issue of Pop...nevertheless, Celia had never been happier.

But one look at Nate suggested he wasn't feeling the same. His eyes had dark circles and his hair was looking slightly unkempt. No big deal for most men, but Nate took great pride in his appearance.

Uh-oh. Maybe things weren't going so well in Mandyland, after all.

"Hey, Celia," he said as he shut the door behind him. "I hope it's okay if I drop by."

While she had seen her ex-husband a handful of times in town since he had helped with Pop after the fire, not one of those incidents had been inside the cupcake shop. In fact, he'd never been inside her business.

"Of course," she said warmly. She had been hurt when he left, but truth be told, it was the best thing that could have happened to her. She swept out her hands proudly, gesturing to the amazing place she'd created. "Welcome to Cee-cee's Cupcakes."

A tired smile spread across his face. "I remember when you used to make cupcakes when the kids were younger."

Before he'd practically banned sugar in their house. Back when she'd let him run their lives. But why was he bringing that up?

He hesitated, then said, "You look great, Cee-cee."

Nate hadn't called her Cee-cee in years. He'd thought it too childlike and unsophisticated. In fact, the last time she'd heard it from his lips had been back when they were newly married. And she hadn't seen that gleam in his eyes since back then either.

Oh.

"Thanks," she said carefully. "Happiness will do that."

If he had given her that look soon after he left her, she might have jumped back into their marriage headfirst without even a second thought. But in her new life, she was thankful he hadn't. She felt absolutely nothing for this man, other than a gentle sort of fondness because the sweep of his long nose reminded her of their son, Gabe, and his smile was so like Max's. He was the father of her kids, but nothing more.

"I heard you were entering the East Coast Holiday Cupcake Battle," he said, changing the subject to something that felt less loaded than her appearance.

She lifted her brow in surprise. "And where did you hear that?"

"Mandy heard it from Maryanne Brown, who heard it from Nina Peterson," he said with a smirk. Small-town gossip was very real in Bluebird Bay.

Celia knew that Amanda was great friends with Maryanne, who was a cousin of Nina Peterson's, the owner of the cookie shop by the pier. Celia and Nina had gone out for coffee last week and they'd discussed the contest.

She forced a grin, preparing herself for Nate's forthcoming lecture about being practical and not following pipe dreams, reminding herself that it was none of his business, in any case. "That's right. There's a fifty-thousand-dollar prize and just finaling could get the shop a lot of great publicity."

"I'm really proud of you, Cee-cee. You've followed your dreams. The cupcake shop suits you."

Celia nearly swallowed her tongue. What would she have given to hear him say that even a year ago? "How are you doing?"

She cared about his well-being but stopped short of asking about Amanda.

He shrugged. "Okay…"

The way he said it suggested he wasn't okay and that he was waiting for her to press him for an answer.

"How's work going?" she asked before she could stop herself. "I heard you sold the warehouse south of town."

"Yeah," he said absently. "I did."

He was staring at her with a moony look, like he wanted to take an emotional stroll down memory lane. She needed to derail this quick.

"You here for a cupcake?" she asked a little too brightly. "Crazy day today, so we don't have a lot left to choose from, but I'll give you one on the house." The sooner she could get him out the door, the better. She had a feeling he was either about to tell her their divorce was a mistake or break out into a lengthy explanation of how awful his day had been. She was interested in neither, and if he persisted, she'd be put in the awkward position of telling him it wasn't her problem anymore.

His gaze dropped to the bakery case. "Uh…thanks." He pointed to the top row. "Cookies and cream."

"Good choice," she said.

His gaze lifted to hers. "Reminds me of how it used to be. When the kids were small."

She quickly pulled the cupcake from the case. "To go?"

Understanding filled his eyes. "Yeah." Clearing his throat, he said, "How's Pop and everyone doing?"

A loaded question if there ever was one, after that debacle at Thanksgiving yesterday. Luckily, in spite of her father's attempts to shove his antiquated beliefs on them all, and her nephew's efforts to get him to change his ways this late in life, the day hadn't been a total loss. The meal had been delicious, and Anna's arrival had been a blessing. The evening had ended on a very sweet note when Sarah's boyfriend, Oliver, had gotten down on one knee in front of everyone and proposed. All in all, not the worst holiday, she supposed.

But Cee-cee was fairly certain Nate was referring specifically to Pop's mental health in the wake of the fire, so she kept her answer vague.

"He's cantankerous as always." Grabbing a preassembled box, she set the cupcake inside, then added another. "He's driving Stephanie crazy, but I'm hoping now that all three of us are here in town, it will take some of the pressure off." If Anna stuck around long enough to pitch in once her ribs healed, at least.

The bell on the front door dinged as Nate responded. "Yeah, I heard Anna was back in town. Why so early? Max had mentioned she was going to be gone almost until Christmas."

"Funny," Anna said as she walked through the front door. "I didn't realize you cared about my comings and goings, Nate."

Her tone was borderline snippy, but Celia couldn't help grinning at her sister. Celia might have gotten past Nate's betrayal, but Anna certainly hadn't, not that she'd ever liked him much anyway.

His eyes widened, looking very much like a kid with his hand in the cookie jar—even if he was reaching for a cupcake.

Anna laughed at his mortified expression. "Cat got your tongue, Nate? Or maybe Amanda's got that in her purse, along with other parts of your anatomy?"

His face reddened and he turned back to Celia and snatched the box out of her hand. "Good seeing you, Cee-cee."

Then he bolted past Anna and out the door.

Anna burst out laughing, then groaned and pressed her hand to her left side. "Oww!"

"Serves you right," Celia teased, then checked the time. Since she only had a few cupcakes left, she could pawn them off on Anna and get ready for her date with Mick to the Christmas tree-lighting ceremony.

"He's just too easy..." Her grin spread. "And now that you're not together, I can take the potshots I've been holding onto for years."

Celia shook her head. "You're incorrigible."

"And that's why you love me," Anna said.

Celia grabbed the remaining cupcakes from the case. "You're just in time," she said as she locked the front door and turned the sign around. "I'm packing up the last few cupcakes for you."

"My lucky day," Anna said, shuffling to the counter.

"You should be in bed, Anna," Celia scolded. "What are you doing walking around?"

"I can't stay cooped up in my apartment all day. And I wanted a cupcake."

"Then I guess it's my lucky day too. With you taking the last of the cupcakes, I can go get ready for my date with Mick," Celia said. "We're going to the tree-lighting ceremony."

"Oh!" Anna squealed. "I haven't been to one of those in decades."

Anna had never been big on homey traditions, so that was no surprise, but now wasn't the time to start. Celia gave her sister a stern look. "I don't think you should go. And I honestly think you should skip Steph's adoption event Sunday as well. There's bound to be a crowd at both. You might get jostled or elbowed. You're not even supposed to be up and around much."

"I don't need another doctor, Cee-cee. I actually came by to see if you'll go with me to Steph's first yoga class next Monday."

Celia's gaze jerked to hers. "Oh. I completely forgot."

"So?" Anna said. "You can still come, right?"

Celia shook her head with a wince as her to-do list ran through her mind. "I can't. I've got to get ready for the baking challenge."

"That's news to me," Anna said, crossing her arms over her chest. "And besides, it's Stephanie's first class. We need to be there to support her."

Celia pointed her finger at her sister. "With those ribs, *you* shouldn't be doing yoga at all. And for that matter, you wouldn't have been here anyway. You weren't due to come back for two weeks."

"Details!" Anna said.

Celia shook her head. "Well, I can't go. I've got a conference call with the baking challenge coordinator."

Anna looked ticked, but then she pasted a half-smile on her face. "By the way, I've got an amazing flavor idea for you to try with your cupcakes. It's something one of the researchers came up with on my trip."

"And I am totally excited to hear all about it, and your trip, but it's going to have to wait," Celia said. "Tilly hasn't been out in hours and I've got to get ready for my date. How about I call you tomorrow and we can have a gab session?"

Anna started to say something, then stopped and crossed her arms, which drew a grunt of pain. "So I'll have your undivided attention from 6:00 to 6:05 p.m. tomorrow? Thanks for squeezing me in, Bezos." She rolled her eyes and spun around.

"Anna," Celia called after her. "Don't be like that."

But Anna was already out the door.

Well, crud.

She watched her sister hobble down the street and blew out a sigh.

"You can't be everything for everyone and still take care of yourself and your own needs, Cee-cee," she reminded herself sternly as she began to wipe down the countertops.

The Sullivan family's dysfunctional Thanksgiving dinner had been a great reminder that she couldn't fix everything for everybody. That was the old Cee-cee's M.O. New Cee-cee was all about balance. And fifty grand plus the resulting media coverage could balance the crap out of her life. While she was mostly doing this for the exposure—how could she expect to win against more experienced bakeries?—she couldn't help daydreaming about winning. She'd love to give Gabe and Sasha money for their upcoming wedding…She lifted her chin with renewed determination.

Winning had to be her primary focus for the next few weeks. Until then, everyone would just have to take a number and deal with it, because Cee-cee's Cupcakes was about to be the East Coast Holiday Cupcake Battle first-prize winner.

Come hell or high water.

Chapter Five

Anna shuffled down the sidewalk, her gait still irritatingly stilted as she headed through the quaint downtown area toward Max's bookstore. Several women in the midst of painting pottery eyed her through the window of the ceramics shop as she passed, and she made a mental note to wear her sunglasses at all times from now on. The grayish, gloomy weather today didn't merit them, and the sun was already almost set, but it beat having strangers give her that pitying look like she was the victim of an abusive man who'd tenderized her face like a hunk of too-tough beef.

Little did they know, it was only her own insatiable curiosity to blame for the lumps and bumps.

"That's what happens if you go off gallivanting to dangerous places."

She could still hear Pop now, going off on her anew every fifteen minutes or so about all the things she'd done wrong that had resulted in her injuries.

Halfway through coffee and dessert, she'd finally snapped.

"At least I didn't burn my dang house down!"

Even now, she winced thinking about it. If she'd taken a second to consider her words before she'd said them, she might have held back, but Anna was more of a doer than a think-it-through kind of gal. Luckily, while her father had initially looked wounded by the jab, he'd forgotten about it moments later and dug into his pumpkin pie like it never happened. The one and only good thing about a loved one having short-term memory issues.

If only *she* could forget she'd said it as easily...

Between that and her snippy exchange with Cee-cee at the cupcake shop, she was in a bad mood as she approached Mo's Diner. Maybe a piping hot cup of coffee and something sweet would take the edge off.

She stepped inside and headed straight for the dessert case, wrinkling her nose at the offerings. Three slices of a carrot cake that looked like it had peaked sometime around Halloween, a sad slice of red velvet with a thumbprint in the cream cheese frosting, and a bunch of glazed donuts with most of the glaze chipped off.

"They came in like rabid wolves around lunchtime and cleaned us out of pretty much everything. Your sister's cupcakes were gone by noon," Eva remarked with a snort as she bustled toward the counter, swiping her hands on her apron as she eyed Anna expectantly. "We still have some pot roast in the back. You want?"

Eva Hildebrand had lived in Bluebird Bay her whole life, and nothing happened in this town without Eva knowing about it. Which probably explained why she didn't even blink at Anna's bruised face as she continued.

"I set an order aside for your daddy already and am bringing it over after my shift is done, but there is just enough for a second..."

"No, thanks, Eva. I'll just take two large coffees and a couple of those donuts to go," Anna replied.

Max was known far and wide for her less than glamorous palate, with her all-time favorite food being the humble tuna melt, so she wouldn't turn her nose up at an ugly donut. Especially not if it came with a coffee to dunk it in. Still, Anna couldn't help but regret her decision to storm indignantly out of Cee-cee's without at least snagging a few cupcakes first, and going back now would surely take the drama out of her exit...

A good flounce always came at a price, she reminded herself with a martyr's sigh as Eva rang up her order.

"That'll be five fifty."

She dug the cash out of her purse and handed it over, along with a dollar tip for Eva.

"Be back in a flash," the older woman said as she headed toward the coffee station.

Anna nodded and cocked a hip against the counter as she waited.

"My, my, my, don't you look a mess," a low voice cooed in a grating mix of mock sympathy and poorly disguised glee.

Anna gnawed on the inside of her cheek, mentally counting to ten as she turned to face Maryanne Brown. The woman had been her nemesis since high school, but the start of their rivalry was still a bit of a mystery to Anna. She didn't let that pesky detail stop her from participating in it wholeheartedly, though.

"Hello, Maryanne. And——" She eyed the balding but fit, middle-aged male beside her for a long moment before shaking her head as if nonplussed. "Steve? Or Bill? Sorry, which one are you? I lost track after husband number three."

"Reggie," the guy replied, a smile tugging at the corner of his lips. "I don't have a number yet, but a guy can dream."

A laugh bubbled from Anna's lips and she found herself sort of liking poor Reggie. At least he had a sense of humor. Apparently, Maryanne still didn't though, because she gut-checked him with a stiff elbow. He let out a muffled *ooph* as she stepped closer to Anna with a tight smile.

"I guess not even knocking yourself senseless and looking a dreadful mess can make you less cocky. Must be freeing to be that delusional, but in case no one has taken pity on you and told you yet, allow me to be the first. You shouldn't go out in public looking like that. I know that I, for one, have lost my appetite just looking at those grisly bruises." She shuddered, her slim shoulders shaking as she took a step back. "Come on, Reggie, let's go. I'm not hungry anymore."

"Probably for the best," Anna said with a sage nod as Eva came back with two steaming to-go cups. "I think the diner is fresh out of souls anyway, Maryanne. You crazy kids have a lovely evening."

Anna shoved the bag of donuts into her oversized purse and took the cups from a grinning Eva before making her way out of the diner, leaving Maryanne glaring after her.

So long as the woman kept her attacks focused on Anna alone and didn't involve her sisters, she usually didn't let it affect her mood. Today, though, the verbal sparring only made an already crappy day feel even worse. The real kicker of it was, Maryanne was probably right. Anna really should lie low until she looked less like a creature from a horror movie and felt better, but she was too stir-crazy to sit at home. If she scared some of the townsfolk, so be it.

She continued toward the bookstore, her ribs aching a little more with each step. Moving for too long hurt, but sitting still for too long was going to drive her batty. Nobody needed that much time alone with their thoughts, least of all Anna. It was a recipe for misery and rash decisions.

The swirling thoughts about her career that had kept her up the night before threatened to rush back in, and she shoved them away, tightening her grip on the hot cups in her hands.

"Sore ribs it is," she mumbled as she reached the door of the bookstore. She pushed it open with the toe of her boot and ambled in.

She found Max sitting at the counter, book in hand.

"Aunt Anna!" Her niece slid off her perch and set the paperback down with a wide smile. "Bearing gifts, no less. Excellent!"

She took one of the cups and rounded the counter, leading Anna over to a little reading nook.

"I was stir-crazy, so I decided to go for a little walk and stop by to see my favorite niece."

Max rolled her eyes as they both sat. "You realize Sarah and I figured out long ago that you call us both that, depending on who you're talking to, right?"

"I plead the Fifth," Anna chirped, digging into the donut bag and plucking one out before handing it to Max. "Be forewarned, these are end-of-the-day leftovers from Mo's, so don't get your hopes up."

Max bit into hers with a happy sigh. "Don't care," she mumbled around the treat. "I haven't eaten since lunch and all I had was soup. This is fabulous."

"You're a cheap date like your auntie." Anna took a pull from her steaming cup before leaning forward with a wince and setting it down.

"You've overdone it. I can see it in your face. I'm open for another—" Max paused to glance at her watch, "—

thirty-five minutes today. Then I'm driving you back to your place. You've done enough walking for today."

"Fine, fine," Anna said, settling back into the seat. "I won't argue. Speaking of the business, how's it going here?"

Max's smooth forehead furrowed and she took another bite of her donut before replying. "Don't tell mom, but not awesome. Don't get me wrong," she hurried to add, tucking a strand of long, dark hair behind one ear, "I love it. Every single day I walk into the shop and smell the books, and see how happy the customers that *do* come in are when I have something they want. I feel like I'm where I'm meant to be, but my bank account says differently."

"Are you short? Do you need a loan?" Anna asked, studying Max's face with concern. Anna only had herself to rely on financially as she crept toward retirement, but she'd also only had herself to take care of all these years. She'd always made sure to be aggressive as far as savings were concerned. If her niece needed her help, she would happily give it. Max might be floundering right now, but she had a good head on her shoulders.

"No, I'm okay for the short term, but thank you for the offer," she said, leaning in to give Anna's hand a grateful squeeze. "My apartment is super cheap with the whole roommate-sharing-expenses situation, which is working out great. And I've got enough to get the bookstore through the rest of this year and half of next even if I don't turn a dime of profit. But after that? I'm toast. The time to right this ship is now. Hey! You're in town for a while, right?"

Anna nodded. "I'm not sure how long, but it will be at least a few months before I can travel comfortably."

"Want to do a coffee table book of your photographs? I'm really good with graphics and can format the whole thing for you. Just think"—she held up her hands like she was framing a sign—*"Local artist and bookstore owner join forces to release a visual love letter to Bluebird Bay.* You probably have a billion shots of the ocean and the lighthouse and the wildlife. It would just be a matter of selecting them and putting it together. We can do a signing here and everything. What do you say?"

A project that wouldn't require her to crawl around on the ground, but which would keep her brain busy while she recuperated? Sounded like a gift from the heavens above. "I say yes! That sounds like so much fun. Tourists that come would probably love it as a keepsake, especially if we price it right."

"And they can each be signed by the photographer! So cool," Max said, visibly excited by the prospect. "It's just taken me a while to accept the fact that people want more than just books. Especially during the off-season. Now I just need something to get the townies in here and coming back. Like they do at the diner, or Mom's shop."

"And what do those places have in common?" Anna asked slowly.

"Well, Mo's has been here forever. It's like an institution, and their blue-plate specials are great. Mom's place is new, but her cupcakes are to die for—" She broke off and then sat back with a chuckle. "Food. Food and drink. But people bring coffee and snacks in all the time when they come…"

"Exactly. So if they come, browse, read for a while and then leave, you've made zero money. If they come in and buy your coffee and your snacks, then at least you've made a profit there. Do you know the margin on coffee at those fancy shops is like 91% per cup? Do yourself a favor. Invest in a big brewing station, amazing coffee beans, and some gourmet snacks. I bet you things will really turn around."

Max's eyes lit up. "Mom gives Mo's a wholesale deal. I bet I can have her do the same for me. Muffins, so they're less messy and easier to eat while you read, maybe? Something a little different...even exclusive to the bookstore!"

Max's enthusiasm was catchy, and soon enough, the two of them were planning all sorts of fun names for coffee drinks and muffin flavors.

They'd come up with more than a dozen book-themed muffin flavors, like "The Lemony Snicket," and Anna's suggestion of "Winter is Coming," a peppermint mocha combo for the holiday season. The two were still on a roll with ideas when Max's face dimmed.

"Guh, I just realized, this is going to have to wait until after Christmas. Mom is in the middle of this Cupcake Battle thing. Between that and Mick, and her shifts with Pop, she really doesn't have time for this..."

It didn't take much for Anna to read between the lines and fill in the rest of Max's thought. The unspoken words *or anyone else* hung in the air between them.

"I'm really happy for her," Max continued, toying with the crumpled bag between them. "And Mick is clearly crazy about her. I just miss hanging out with her. Seems like she has enough time to grill me about the bookstore, the guy I'm dating, and if I'm eating right, but she doesn't have enough time to just talk. It sucks a bit, that's all."

"You're dating someone? Do tell."

Max's cheeks went pink and Anna grinned.

"His name is Robbie. He's, uh, he's a bit of a rebel. Kind of wild. I think that's why Mom's worried. Leather jacket. Long, black hair. Piercing green eyes. Dastardly dimple. He's an artist. He makes wrought iron sculptures— Aunt Anna, they're amazing. I won't lie, he looks like trouble and he's definitely intense, but he's got a heart of gold..." Max's smile faded. "Which Mom wouldn't know about because she's only met him once, and can't spare an evening to meet up with us for dinner to get to know him."

"Well, I think he sounds awesome, and I can't wait to meet him. I'm glad you're finally getting out there."

"Me too, and that sounds great. We'll make a plan to get a bite to eat so I can introduce you. I'm sure he'd love to see your photos."

Max seemed happy about the three of them getting together, but while Anna's approval was nice, it wasn't required. Fact of the matter was, as close as she and Max were, Anna wasn't her mom. She made a mental note to test the waters with Cee-cee on the whole Robbie and Max topic when they spoke tomorrow evening.

It was tough, because she could tell that her oldest sister was having the time of her life. Anna was so happy for her. But she was also a little jealous. Not because she wanted what Cee-cee had or begrudged her anything, but because part of her missed the coddling Cee-cee of days past. Even six months ago, if Anna had come home early after a long trip—especially after a serious fall—Cee-cee would have dropped everything to mother-hen her and make her chicken soup and spend time with her. Instead, she'd penciled Anna in for a call, like a client.

"It's weird, isn't it?" she mused with a bittersweet smile. "When I saw your mom today and she didn't drop everything for me, I was hurt. All these years, I've been telling her she needs to find her passion and stop putting other people before herself. It's a tough pill to swallow that I apparently didn't mean me."

"Me too," Max said with a shamefaced chuckle. "And me neither. Maybe it's because we're the babies of the family and we're used to being fawned over."

Anna held her now-lukewarm cup aloft. "Bratty baby sisters, unite."

Max tapped her cup against Anna's. "Here's to piping down and growing up, I guess."

Anna took a sip of her coffee and nodded to herself. Nothing was even actually wrong. Everything just seemed magnified to her right now because of her injury. Usually, she'd come home from a trip feeling energized, fulfilled, and happy for the break. This time was different. This time, she felt old, tired, and lonelier than she ever remembered. It wasn't Cee-cee's fault she needed her more than usual. Anna had to adjust her expectations of her sister and remember how much better Cee-cee's life was now that she and Nate were apart and Cee-cee was living her dream.

This was good. Cathartic, even. The first step toward making a change was acknowledging the problem. She had something to do now, with the whole bookstore project, and this little thing with her and Cee-cee would be fine. They'd catch up on their one-on-one call tomorrow, see each other at Steph's adoption event on Sunday, and be as close as ever.

Easy peasy, no problem.

Chapter Six

Stephanie looked around the Bluebird Bay Community Center, flushed with excitement. When she'd heard that the chamber of commerce was having a Christmas festival, she immediately suggested an adoption event. When her kids heard about it, they were eager to jump on board and help, not that she was surprised. Pet adoption events had been one of her kids' favorite parts of her profession. Cee-cee and Mick had agreed to help, and Eva had gotten the night off from the diner to make sure Pop behaved himself. Gabe and Sasha were also there along with a subdued Max. Anna had come too, even though she still looked like she'd been in an MMA fight and lost, despite Anna having slathered on a generous layer of concealer and foundation. Multiple pens were set up around the rec room, containing freshly washed and groomed dogs wearing a variety of holiday kerchiefs and ribbons, as well as cats in stacked wire cages. They also had a wide variety of dog and cat toys, collars, and leashes, along with a wrapping station set up for children to wrap gifts for their family pets. Jeff, Stephanie's youngest son, had brought his nice digital camera and had set up an area with a Christmas tree next to a fake fireplace to take pet portraits. Stephanie was proud that all proceeds were going to the Bluebird Bay Animal Rescue Group.

When Stephanie walked over to unlock the doors, she was delighted to see there was a line stretched out down the sidewalk, waiting to come in.

The community center quickly filled with a cacophony of voices, and while it was slightly overwhelming, it filled her with happiness. It was no secret she had a heart for animals, and she believed all animals deserved a loving home.

Soon there was a short line at Jeff's photography station, and Max—who was manning the accessories—had a small line of customers to ring up. Everyone else was watching the animals and answering questions about them or calling for Stephanie to answer what they couldn't.

When Anna took a seat next to a pen, it was obvious she'd been pushing too hard. Her face was drawn and pale and she was moving much slower and more gingerly than usual. Stephanie realized that she'd let Anna fool her into thinking her injuries weren't as bad as they looked, but now she was having second thoughts. Stephanie definitely intended to keep an eye on her baby sister.

"Mom," her daughter, Sarah, called out. "Can you talk to this lovely family about Ginger?"

Stephanie walked over, beaming at the parents and their two school-aged kids. "Ginger is a spayed, five-month-old cocker-doodle who was brought into the shelter because her previous owner underestimated how much exercise she needed. Cocker-doodles are cute but they have boundless energy. She'll need plenty of time on walks or romping in the yard with kids. They're great family dogs."

Stephanie bent over to rub Ginger's head and was rewarded with a lick on her lips. She laughed and stood. "And she's obviously very affectionate."

The family seemed enthusiastic about the dog, and Sarah winked at her mother, her cue that Stephanie had worked her magic and could move on.

Stephanie was about to walk toward a couple who were holding a black kitten when she saw Beckett Wright walk through the door. His gaze scanned the room and landed on Anna, who was holding a sleeping puppy on her lap. Beckett headed straight for her.

"Hey, Anna," he said when he reached her.

Anna hadn't seen him walk in, and now her face was flushed. "Beckett...hi."

"Hi," he said with a soft smile. "I heard you were back early. How was the trip?"

"Great," she said with a short laugh, then pressed her arm against her side. "Until the end, anyway. The price of a great photo."

Stephanie narrowed her eyes, noticing her sister hadn't told the tow truck driver how she'd gotten injured.

"So you found the polar bears?" Beckett asked, and Stephanie couldn't help wondering when he and Anna had discussed her assignment.

"I did," Anna said. "And plenty of other animals too. Everything else was a bonus at that point."

"If your photos are anything like the puffin one you gave me," he said, "then I know they are amazing."

Anna had given him a photo from her puffin assignment this summer? Obviously there was a whole lot that had slipped Stephanie's attention. Then again, a lot had slipped her attention for the last two years since Paul had died—something she'd vowed to fix. For starters, she'd finally cleaned out his clothes. She was also making an effort to find a life outside her veterinary practice—she'd renewed her yoga teaching certificate and was teaching her first class on Monday night. She'd made so much progress in the last few months, but as she considered how much of her family's lives she'd missed, she suddenly felt very alone again.

Stephanie left Anna and Beckett alone to chat and walked over to Cee-cee and Mick, who were talking to an older woman about a beagle mix. Cee-cee gave her a smile as she talked to the woman, almost as though she were saying, *I'm not new to the adoption fair gig. I've got this covered.* A quick look at Mick cued her in that he was loving this too.

More people poured in, and Stephanie realized that Pop was barking orders at several kids who were wrapping gifts.

"You're using too much tape!" he shouted. "Do you think it's made on trees?"

They looked up at him with wide eyes, and their parents looked like they were about ready to bolt. Not exactly a great impression.

Stephanie sighed. How had Pos made his way over to the gift wrapping station? Stephanie had positioned him next to the cats. She made a beeline toward him, but Eva reached him first.

"Don't you mind this cranky old man," Eva told the kids as she grabbed Pop's long-sleeved, flannel-covered arm. "You use as much tape as you want." Eva then turned to waggle a finger at Pop. "You leave those kids alone," Eva said in a stern tone. "You're spoiling their fun."

"Since when is it fun to waste things?"

"They're kids, Red Sullivan," she snapped. "Your job is to watch over the cats, not police the tape."

Pop crossed his arms over his barrel chest, clearly not happy at his reassignment.

Eva glanced up at Stephanie, and Steph mouthed *thank you*.

Stephanie had no idea where she would mentally be if not for Eva's help and intervention over the last few months, but Stephanie knew she was at her wits' end. She and the kids had spent a glorious, Pop-free day the day before, and two things were becoming crystal clear—there was no way Pop would be going back to his house when it was done, and he needed to move out of Stephanie's house ASAP.

She knew that made her a bitch, but she needed her sanity and her house back. She'd give it until New Year's, but then Pop had to go.

Chapter Seven

Anna stood outside the front door of the community center and shivered as a gust of autumn wind rolled past. It was only six p.m., but a fat, golden moon hung high in the star-studded sky.

"Did you need Mick and me to give you a ride home?"

She turned to find Cee-cee standing behind her, slipping her coat on as Mick chatted with Steph in the doorway.

Anna bit her lip and shook her head. "No, thanks. Beckett has actually offered to take me." Cee-cee had barely given her the time of day since she'd strolled in an hour before, and Anna wanted to say more, like *And you care now, because...?* But she wasn't about to make a scene. Steph had put on an incredible event that had resulted in thirty-six animals finding their forever homes, and if anyone needed a successful, drama-free day, it was Steph. But there was no denying Anna was all in her feelings with Cee-cee right now.

"Okay, are you sure? We don't mind..."

Again, Anna bit back a sharp retort, settling on a half-smile and a shake of her head. "All set, but thank you."

Cee-cee frowned, eyeing her more closely as Anna tried to maintain a poker face.

"What's up with you? You seem off...Are you just sore from all the standing?" Cee-cee huffed out a sigh. "I told you it was best if you didn't come. Anna, if you go to that yoga thing tomorrow—"

"Why didn't you call me last night?"

The words were out before she could stop them and she winced. Yuck. She sounded like a jealous ex begging for scraps. So not her M.O., but it was out there now, nothing to do but see it through.

Cee-cee blinked and then stilled. "Oh my gosh, I totally forgot. Crap, Anna. I'm sorry. I was testing a bunch of new recipes, and trying to write everything down, and it totally slipped my mind. Let me and Mick bring you home so we can talk in the truck for a while, at least."

Anna shrugged and plucked an imaginary lint ball from her pants as she blew out a sigh. This was silly. She wasn't a child in need of hand-holding. She'd just missed her sisters more than usual when she'd been away. That was no excuse to punish Cee-cee for having a life.

"Like I said, Beckett offered to take me home. No big deal, anyway. I just wanted to tell you about that flavor combo my friend came up with in Alaska and stuff. Seriously, I'm being an emotional baby. Let's make a coffee date for a day later this week. How does that sound?"

Cee-cee's eyes narrowed as she dug around in her purse. "Sure. Let me check what day is good. I am meeting with suppliers Tuesday, and then I have the decorating class on Tuesday afternoon." She peered down at the backlit screen and blanched. "Thursday's actually not good either. Um..."

"It's fine, Cee-cee. Do what you have to do, and when you have a chance, have your people call my people and we'll set something up."

She'd meant it to come off as funny, but instead it had sounded flip and a little bitter.

Double crap.

"Cee-cee…"

Before she could think of what to say beyond that, Mick stepped out and slipped an arm around her sister's shoulders. "All set, ladies?"

"Actually, Anna's going home with Beckett, so it's just the two of us," Cee-cee replied. The glow she'd been rocking pretty much nonstop since she'd started working on the cupcake shop seemed to dim just a little as she tucked herself beneath Mick's arm and gave Anna a sad smile. "Look, I'll call you tomorrow after I close the shop, okay?"

Anna nodded, saved from further awkward conversation as Beckett pulled up in his flatbed and Cee-cee and Mick headed toward the parking lot.

Beckett hopped out and went around to open the door and help her in. "I was thinking, do you have dinner plans?"

"Not unless you count heating up a can of Chef Boyardee Beefaroni and watching Golden Girls reruns as a plan."

"If you're not too tired, I haven't eaten either…"

Anna gingerly tugged her seatbelt on and fastened it, shoving her worries aside. She and Cee-cee would figure it out. They always did. She was tired, sore, and hungry, and a super-nice, handsome guy had just asked her out to dinner. It was time to unwind and have a little fun in this town.

"I'm starving. I'd love to."

***

"So, what I'm hearing is that this whole mess could've been avoided, but for your weak bladder."

Anna laughed and then groaned, clutching at her aching ribs. "That's one ungentlemanly way of putting it, yes," she replied.

She didn't know how it happened. They'd been sitting by the crackling fire at The Seaside Shanty working their way through thick, creamy seafood chowder served in sourdough bread bowls and a bottle of Bordeaux when Beckett had somehow charmed the truth out of her.

Part of her thought it might be the atmosphere. They'd managed to snag a table facing the water and the view was astounding, punctuated by white-capped, foamy waves pounding against the craggy shoreline. Between that, the wine, and the cozy fire, she'd have given up government secrets if she'd had any. But there was no denying that part of it was Beckett. It was just so…easy with him. She'd seen his tow truck in town over the years, but she'd only actually met him in person shortly before her trip to Alaska. It was strange how comfortable she felt with him. Like they'd been friends for years.

"Really, though, I'm glad it wasn't more serious. I'm sure this is a major nuisance, but it could've been a lot worse."

She nodded and tore off a hunk of sourdough. "Agreed. I was thinking the same thing when it happened. I could've broken my fool neck out there." She made a mental note to make an appointment with Dr. Waverly for a follow-up to make sure things were healing as they should be, and then turned her attention back to Beckett. "I feel like all we've done is talk about my work and my trip. Tell me about you. What do you do when you're not dislodging people's cars from snow banks and such?"

Beckett set down his spoon and swiped at his mouth with his napkin. "Let's see, I've got a six-month old grandson named Tommy who I'm pretty crazy about. I try to get him overnight every couple of weeks. I play poker with some buddies of mine every Tuesday night. And, thanks to your inspiration, I've actually started taking pictures."

Anna blinked at him and swallowed the hunk of bread lodged in her throat. She knew she should be focusing on his other hobbies, especially his newly minted one as it was a common thread, but instead, only one word stood out in her mind, like a neon sign.

"Grandson, huh? That's so nice!" And also oddly terrifying.

It wasn't that weird. She was forty-eight, after all, and Beckett looked to be in his early fifties. Tons of people had grandkids at that age. But suddenly, the warmth of the fire felt cloying and the creamy chowder seemed to curdle in her stomach.

"Um, can you excuse me? I've just got to run to the ladies' room."

Beckett stood as she did, gaze locked on her as she scurried away. It wasn't until she was behind the ladies' room door that she let out the pent-up breath she'd been holding.

A grandson.

"Stop it, you idiot. It's just dinner. It's not like you've suddenly inherited a grandchild or something," she mumbled under her breath as she rushed to the sink and ran the faucet. But, like everything with her lately, it wasn't so much about Beckett or his little bundle of joy. It was about her. Anna Sullivan. And the fact that, no matter how hard she tried to pretend otherwise, she was getting older.

"Almost fifty," she said out loud at her reflection as she let the cool water run over her wrists and hands. She'd been having weird hot flashes like this a lot lately. In fact, her last week in Alaska, she'd felt so off and out of sorts she'd feared she'd caught the flu. Now, though, as she peered at herself in the mirror, it all began to make sense. The exhaustion, the heightened emotions.

Menopause.

She let out a groan and then squinted, leaning closer to the mirror.

No way. No freaking way.

But upon further inspection, there was no denying it. Mixed in with her unruly auburn mop, it glowed like a beacon, mocking her.

One long, gray hair.

"No, no, no..." she muttered as she gripped it and started to tug before stopping herself. It might be an old wives' tale, but she could've sworn she remembered someone telling her that if you pulled a gray hair out, three came back in its place. And the only thing worse than your first gray hair was a crap-ton more of them.

She turned off the water and wheeled away from the mirror, chock-full of determination and the almost manic optimism that only a few glasses of red wine could bring.

Fine. It was totally fine. So what if her sisters had both been blessed with silky, gorgeous locks and hers had been a frizzy mess and not having any grays had been her one and only claim to hair fame? Didn't matter. She was still the same person. Fun-loving, physically fit, adventure-seeking Anna. The cool aunt. The bon vivant. The same old never-stay-in-one-place, grab-life-by-the-twig-and-berries-and-squeeze Anna. And as soon as she was all healed up, she'd prove it.

But as she made her way back toward her date, a shiver of unrest rolled through her. Something told her things were about to get a lot more complicated.

Chapter Eight

O h," Cee-cee moaned as she sank into the couch and closed her eyes, her legs sprawled over Mick's lap at the opposite end. He was massaging the balls of her feet and it felt heavenly.

"Where have you been all of my life?" she asked, letting herself relax for the first time since she'd woken before the sun rose.

"Waiting for you here in Bluebird Bay," he murmured, moving to her arch.

His words were playful, but they caught her attention. She partially sat up. "What?"

Mick had had a crush on her in high school, and she on him, but he'd never acted on it because he'd always planned to stay to work for his father in his construction business, and Mick had known that Cee-cee wanted to go to college and possibly move away. They'd wanted different things, and even as a kid, Mick had been mature enough to respect that. What she'd said was thoughtless.

When he saw the alarm in her eyes, he gave her a soft smile. "I was teasing."

He picked up her other foot and started massaging.

While Mick *had* been here, he hadn't been waiting for her—he'd lived his life—and she was so lucky that he'd still been available when her marriage ended. Of course, Cee-cee had heard the whispers of people suggesting she was getting too involved with him too soon. But while she hated being the subject of gossip, hated people knowing her personal business, she reminded herself that it was part and parcel not only of living in a small town, but of being a small business owner too.

Cee-cee didn't want to think about what other people were saying. She chose to focus on the future…and more specifically the East Coast Holiday Cupcake Battle, which had become an all-consuming part of her life.

Mick must have read her mind. "How'd your latest call with the baking challenge coordinator go?"

"Good," she said, her eyes closing again. Tilly was lying on her dog bed next to the sofa, and her soft snores made Cee-cee smile. "She explained the rules in depth."

"Why do you look so worried?" he asked.

She popped one eye open to silently question him.

He grinned. "Your forehead gets two deep wrinkles across the middle when you're fretting about something."

Wrinkles. She self-consciously reached her hand to her forehead. She was fifty-two, and while she looked young for her age, the effects of time and sun were evident on her face. Even if they surprised her more and more when she looked in the mirror.

Mick grabbed her wrist and tugged her to a sitting position next to him. "Sorry. Shouldn't have mentioned it."

"It's okay," she said, forcing a smile.

"No," he said carefully, dropping her foot and turning so they were eye to eye, a little over a foot apart. "It's not if what I said made you self-conscious about how you look."

Tenderness filled his eyes. "You're beautiful, Cee-cee, inside and out. Wrinkles and all. My favorite sight in the entire world is you."

She was about to call him out for feeding her lines, but the adoration in his eyes proved he meant every word. She dropped her gaze. "Thanks."

He carefully placed a finger under her chin and lifted her gaze to meet his. "I love you, Celia Burrows."

Her breath caught in her throat. Every declaration of love from this man felt like he was saying it for the first time. "I love you too."

He leaned forward and gave her a gentle kiss, reassuring her that he did love her, wrinkles and all. When he pulled away, he smiled. "Now, about the rules for that contest…"

She pushed out a sigh. "This competition is going to take so much time. More time than I realized. It's going to be all-consuming."

"And you're worried about spending so much time on something you want to do versus what other people think you should be doing?"

She opened her mouth to answer him, stopped, then restarted, reminded once again of how well he knew her. "Well, yeah. It feels selfish. Pop is getting more difficult to handle, Anna just turned up with injuries from her trip. Christmas is around the corner—my kids' first Christmas with me and Nate not together. And then there's you…"

"What about me?" he asked, his tone turning serious.

"It's not fair to ask you to give up so much of your time to this contest, from hearing me talk about it incessantly to creating my display stands for each round." She gave him a tiny shrug. "It's a lot."

"First of all," he said, wrapping an arm loosely around her lower back and tugging her closer, "you've spent your entire life taking care of everyone else, and before you deny it, can I remind you that I've lived in the same small town with you. I've seen you in action. Everyone and everything came before Celia Burrows."

She grimaced. "Guilty as charged."

"There is absolutely nothing wrong with you starting to live your own life and putting your own needs and wants first. Your kids are grown and living their own lives. Pop is your sisters' father too. And as for me, I'm exactly where I want to be, with the person I want to be with, doing exactly what I want to do." A sexy gleam filled his eyes. "Well, almost everything, but we can take care of *that* later."

She chuckled. "You sure know how to put things into perspective."

"Just one of many reasons to keep me around." He leaned forward and whispered conspiratorially, "I'm not sure if you've heard, but I'm kind of handy."

Cee-cee released a laugh, the delicious euphoria of happiness washing through her. She'd been more joyful in the last four months than she'd likely been her entire life. That was proof enough that she wasn't rushing into anything with Mick. That they were meant to be.

"Now, back to the contest," he said. "The rules please. I need to know my limitations when building your props." He waggled his eyebrows. "See? Purely selfish motives on my part."

She laughed again, then recapped the rules. Bakers had to use original recipes during all three rounds of competition, which would be spread out over three days—half the bakers competing in two rounds on the first day, the other half on the second. The final round would be on the third day. Half the bakers would be eliminated at the end of each first round, then only two would remain after each second round, leaving four finalists. The winner would be chosen at the end of the third round. "We're strongly encouraged to make multiple flavors each round," she said, her throat feeling tight with anxiety.

"So?" he asked tenderly. "You've got dozens of original recipes that people drive twenty miles to try."

Raking her teeth across her bottom lip, she said, "Creamsicle is the absolute favorite of my customers. The shop is becoming known for it. Should I use it first or save the best for last? Presuming I even make it to the final round."

He shook his head. "Put it out there front and center. You'll regret it if you don't go out swinging in the first round. If you're gonna do this, go big or go home, Cee-cee."

She leaned over and gave him a kiss. "You're right."

He grinned against her lips. "I like the sound of that."

Her mind was sorting through her imaginary recipe filing cabinet when she remembered Anna had been trying to tell her about a flavor suggestion.

"Oh!" she exclaimed. "How could I have forgotten again? I was supposed to call Anna, but the shop has been surprisingly busy and planning for the competition, and—"

Mick kissed her to stop her litany, then said, "It's okay. Anna takes off on her trips and you don't hear from her except for the occasional email and sporadic phone calls. She's busy with her job, and now so are you. Anna's spent most of her adult life putting you on hold so she can pursue what she loves, and you cheered her success every step of the way. There's no reason she can't wait for you too."

She frowned. "When you put it that way…"

His eyes lit up. "Feel free to tell me I'm right again."

Laughing, she swatted his chest. "You're terrible."

A playful look swept over his face. "Not the words I was going for, but I can work with that."

Cee-cee's thoughts were still on Anna, though. While she knew Mick was right, being more selfish with her time was still a guilt-inducing process. Old habits died hard. Just because she was finding more time for herself didn't mean she had to give up her sisters too. It just meant balancing her time better, which sounded great in theory, but there were only so many hours in the day, and the shop, the competition, and Mick were sucking up the majority of them. The rest seemed to be soaked up by much-needed sleep. Still, she missed her sister and she wanted to hear more about Anna's trip.

She leaned over and snatched her phone off the table, then pulled up Anna's name and sent her a text.

My life's been crazy, but I'd love to catch up over breakfast on Friday morning at 9. You. Me. Maybe Steph? We can eat our weight in pancakes at Stacks. My treat.

She'd just wake up an hour before her usual time, get all her baking done early, head over to Stacks and have a leisurely breakfast with her sisters before she opened the shop for the day.

Balance.

When Anna didn't answer right away, Cee-cee tried to put it out of her head as she and Mick started discussing her cupcake flavors and which would make the best impression with the judges. Finally, a half hour later, Anna sent back a reply.

Sounds good. See you then.

Cee-cee frowned at the unusually short and to-the-point text. She knew Anna was used to getting Cee-cee's full and nearly undivided attention whenever she wanted it when she was home. But Anna would get used to this new arrangement.

Wouldn't she?

Chapter Nine

S top sulking. It's unbecoming for a forty-eight-year-old woman."

"I'm not sulking," Anna snapped back, frowning at her sister. "I'm...eh, yeah, whatever. I'm sulking," she admitted with a shrug as she hunkered deeper into the passenger's seat of Steph's car. "I just don't see why you have to come to my doctor's appointment. It's literally nothing. A quick checkup to make sure things are healing properly, and that's it."

"Yeah, that's what I want to find out about too. I also have a few questions," Steph said, tightening her grip on the wheel. "I'm a not GP, but I'm a doctor nonetheless and I can't imagine that anyone told you it was a good idea to go to a yoga class with broken ribs. Either you have the stupidest doctors ever, or you can't be trusted to do what you're told."

"I'm not a child, Steph."

"Could've fooled me," her older sister muttered under her breath as they pulled into the parking lot of the doctor's office.

Anna was about to snap back again when she realized her hands were fisted at her sides like the five-year-old she'd seen having a tantrum at the grocery earlier today, which let the air out of her balloon of self-righteousness.

"Oh my God. You hit the nail on the head. You're totally right, Steph. I'm being a big, fat baby," Anna admitted with a sigh, forcing herself to unclench her hands. "I seriously don't know what's wrong with me lately. It's like I knocked something loose in my brain when I fell or something, and I can't seem to make it go back the way it was before. I feel like I'm moving closer and closer to the edge of a cliff. I just want it to…stop. I keep thinking the most maudlin thoughts. My body is betraying me. I get hot flashes, my face seems intent on sliding downward, cute guys are calling me ma'am. I've even got a gray hair," she said, jabbing a finger at the offender. "I've decided to name him Kevin." She turned to her sister. "Steph, what's happening to me?"

Steph slid the car into one of the parking spaces and then slipped it into park before turning to face Anna. "It's scary, isn't it?" she asked softly. "Getting older. It's like, one day you're young and cool and you've got your whole life ahead of you, and then all of a sudden, things start to happen. Your hands hurt when it's cold outside or it's about to rain. You throw your back out doing something super daring like bending down to pick up a sock. You wind up at more funerals than you do weddings…mourning more often than you celebrate. The father you thought was as tough as rawhide starts to unravel right before your eyes. The husband you thought was invincible…isn't." She broke off and Anna had to blink back tears as she waited for her sister to continue. "Getting older is not for the faint of heart, kiddo. All I can say is that you're in good company. Cee-cee and I have had more than a few talks about this kind of stuff. If you ever need to vent or cry, or sulk, I'm always here for you. Even when you don't want me to be."

Steph unclipped her seatbelt and reached out to do the same with Anna's.

"Now come on, let's get your scolding over with, okay? If you're a good girl, Doctor Waverly will give you a sticker and I'll bring you to the cupcake shop for a treat after."

Anna laughed through her tears and shoved the car door open. "I know you're mocking me and I should argue with you, but I could really use a sticker and a cupcake right now, so I'm gonna let it slide."

As annoyed as she'd been initially, as they crunched through the blanket of leaves leading toward the doctor's office, she had to admit that she was kind of glad Steph was there now. Not because she needed a keeper—if Doc Waverly came down on her hard about doing too much, she'd scale back some—but ever since she'd left Alaska, she'd been plain out of sorts and super lonely. What she'd always viewed as "space" and much-needed "alone time" suddenly felt empty and hollow, "peace and quiet" more like "oppressive silence."

And that very train of thought terrified her. It was a threat to her independence and her sense of adventure…everything she'd held dear. The very things that defined her.

So now what?

She thought back to her date with Beckett and winced as she recalled the way it had ended. They'd been having a great time, and then she'd ruined it when she couldn't seem to keep the negative thoughts at bay. By the time dessert came, she was babbling like some old-timey vaudeville act, doing everything but the old soft shoe to entertain, telling joke after joke that felt forced and flat to cover up the insecurity that was threatening to swallow her whole. He'd clearly sensed the switch and when she'd finally run out of gas, he'd taken her home with no mention of a future date or phone call. Not that she could blame him. She'd acted like a certifiable nutcase.

She let out an involuntary groan and Steph gave her a worried look.

"Ribs that sore today?"

"Nope, just my pride," she said with a tight smile as they walked into the homey little office of her primary care physician. She stepped up to the window and waved to the receptionist. "Hi there, Anna Sullivan to see Dr. Waverly."

"She's just finishing up with another patient. I'll let her know you're here."

She and Steph had barely gotten comfortable when a nurse came to get them. She made quick work of checking Anna's weight and vitals before exiting the room and leaving a johnny coat behind, having instructed her to put it on with the opening facing front.

"These things are barbaric," Steph said, wrinkling her nose as Anna began to strip off her leggings and sweater. "Maybe they'd be better in a print."

"Yeah, I'd be okay with the solid blue if I didn't have to have either my butt cheeks or my lady bits hanging out of it," Anna countered as she struggled into the paper dress.

A light rap on the door had her rushing to tie the thing shut, and she called for the doctor to come in.

"Hey there! Long time no see."

The always diplomatic Dr. Regina Waverly managed to deliver the tiny jab with a wide smile and little enough reproach that Anna couldn't take offense. It *had* been a while.

"I know I missed my annual last year, but seriously, all was well…" Until recently, at any rate.

"I heard you were in Alaska. How were the polar bears?" Dr. Waverly asked as she lowered herself onto the rolling stool and glanced at the computer screen where Anna's information was displayed.

"Amazing. I've been going through the pictures the past few days. They're truly magnificent creatures."

"Sounds like you really enjoyed your trip until you took a spill. Want to tell me what happened?"

"She had to pee, went outside and lost her balance, and went flying down a hill, breaking her fall with a tree stump," Steph supplied helpfully.

Anna pursed her lips and nodded. "Yep, that's about the size of it."

"Nothing like a sister to keep you humble." The doctor grinned and stood, gesturing for Anna to climb onto the paper-covered exam table. "Had you been having any balance problems before that? Any dizzy spells or lightheadedness?"

"No," Anna said reflexively. "Actually, yes. Hot flashes, occasional lightheadedness, mood swings. I think it's perimenopause, but that's not why I fell. I slipped on the ice and I wasn't watching where I was going." She grimaced as the doctor parted the front of the gown and let out a low whistle. "Yeah, it looks worse than it is."

"Well, I saw the X-rays the office in Alaska sent over, and it looks exactly as bad as it is. That said, it's one of those injuries that hurts like the dickens for way longer than you want it to but actually heals up pretty well over time."

She probed the area gently and continued to pepper Anna with questions.

Stephanie stayed mostly quiet until the doctor asked if Anna had been keeping her movement to a minimum.

"She came to my yoga class last night. Granted, she only did the most basic moves, but come on…," Steph said with a snort.

Anna scowled at her.

Snitch.

"I guess you're one of those that needs to hear it all said explicitly, then?" the doctor said, arching one black brow. "No yoga." She began ticking prohibited activities off on her fingers. "No yoga, no jogging, no Zumba, or Jazzercise. No skipping, dancing, roller-blading, or hula-hooping. No sex, either. I missed tons of other activities, but suffice to say that if it requires twisting, standing for too long, sitting too long, or any jarring motions, you shouldn't be doing it. Capisce?"

Anna "capisced" all right, but that didn't mean she had to like it. "Roger that."

"Now that we've gotten that out of the way—and Stephanie, thank you for your honest input—I don't think you did any harm so far. Any spots feeling more hot at all, or more tender than before?" she asked as she continued exerting gentle pressure around her ribs and up under her breasts. Anna was about to say no when the doctor's fingers stilled. "Does this hurt when I touch?"

Anna frowned as she pushed and prodded. "No, that doesn't hurt at all," she said as she glanced down at the place where Dr. Waverly's fingers were pushing. It was just an inch higher and to the right of the bruising, where the skin was more of a sickly yellow than the deep purple everywhere else.

The doctor's gaze narrowed as she leaned closer and continued to palpate the rest of her breast tissue and prod beneath her underarms. "Was your last mammogram the one we have on file?" she asked. Her tone was even and as calm as ever, but no delivery could stop the icy shaft of terror that pierced Anna right in the gut.

"I-I...I think so?"

She locked gazes with a stricken-looking Stephanie as they were hurled in tandem back to another time and place. The two of them, along with Cee-cee, hands locked together in a triple vice grip as their mother's white-haired oncologist gave them the verdict.

"We've done all we can. At this point, it's just a matter of making her as comfortable as possible."

Anna's breath came in short gasps as she struggled to sit up straight, pushing the doctor's hands away. "C-can I have some water?" she asked, trying to talk herself down. This was ridiculous. Another overreaction on her part. Nothing had even happened. It was a normal question...one most doctors who doubled as their patient's ob-gyn would ask.

The doctor padded over to the sink and quickly filled a tiny paper cup with filtered water before carrying it back and handing it to her.

"Anna, I didn't mean to alarm you. Truly," the doctor said gently. "But there is a lump that you didn't have at your last exam and we're going to need to get it checked out. Given your family history, the sooner the better. But that doesn't mean it's cancer, all right? It just means we have to be super proactive. It might be nothing. Are you still with me, Anna?"

Anna drained the cup and tried to form a response when Stephanie cut in with the question she hadn't been able to bring herself to utter.

"What does your gut tell you, Dr. Waverly...Does it feel like nothing?"

The long pause was like a ten-ton weight on her chest, and she knew the answer before the doctor spoke.

"I won't lie to you...I don't like the way it feels, but that's not a diagnosis. I'm going to put an order in for a PET scan ASAP. In fact, I'm going to do my best to get you in for tomorrow morning. If there's something to worry about, we'll know about it in the next few days and get on a path to treatment. If there isn't, we can all breathe a sigh of relief and get on with our lives, the sooner the better. Sound good?"

Steph shifted from all-consuming terror right into crisis mode like she did so well, taking charge with a clipped nod. "Sounds good. What do we need to do in preparation for the testing?"

The rest of the visit passed in a blur as the doctor poked at her, as did the rest of the day. There was no sticker. There were no cupcakes. Stephanie brought her home and stayed by her side until it got dark out and Pop called asking about dinner, at which point she begged Anna to come stay at her house. Anna declined. She couldn't face anyone else right now. She'd already sworn Steph to secrecy so she would have time to process it all.

It wasn't until much later that night, alone in her bed, that Anna finally talked herself down. Lots of people had lumps that turned out to be nothing. It was natural for her to be nervous, given their mother's recent death. This was going to be one of those moments they'd look back on and marvel at how they'd worried for nothing. Her dumb bruised ribs would heal, and soon this would just be a bad memory...

Chapter Ten

Y ou know what, old man? If you keep treating people like this, you're not going to have any friends left."

"Hey, I'm just trying to help! If you keep eating those donuts, people are gonna start calling you Crisco…fat in the can. But if you don't care, I don't care either!"

Eva's warning and Pop's scathing retort echoed through the house as Stephanie yanked off her bra and slipped on a pajama top. First order of business tomorrow? Stop at the drugstore and pick up earplugs. They'd been going at it since she stepped foot in the door twenty minutes before. Part of her was convinced Pop enjoyed it. And, for her part, Eva had thick skin, but he was beyond insulting. The last thing Stephanie needed was for the woman to decide she'd had enough and quit. Especially now, when she could barely even think straight for worrying about Anna.

She closed her eyes and blew out a breath as she slid her feet into a pair of slippers. The past couple of days had gone by at snail speed. Tomorrow was Friday and if they didn't get the results of the PET scan Anna had done the day before, they were going to have to go through the weekend like this. Worried and waiting. Even work hadn't taken

Stephanie's mind off it. Maybe it would've been less terrifying if she'd had someone to talk to about it other than Anna herself. Someone to share her fears with. Someone to cry with. But Anna had been adamant. She didn't want anyone else to know until there was something to actually know. At first Stephanie had assumed Anna meant that they weren't to tell the nieces and nephews or Pop. It had become clear pretty quickly that she'd meant Cee-cee as well. Stephanie had hoped that some rest and a little time would soften her stance, but she'd been dead set. If Stephanie spoke to Cee-cee before the results came in, she was to say nothing about the lump.

Nausea rolled through her and she pressed her fingers to her throbbing temples as she thought about the awkward phone call with her older sister at lunchtime. She'd called to check in and see if Stephanie was still planning to meet them for breakfast the next day. Cee-cee was clearly busy— Stephanie could hear the bustle of the shop in the background—and it should've been a nothing call, yet instead of answering her question and saying a quick goodbye, Stephanie had instantly choked up, eyes welling with tears. She'd wound up hanging up and texting a minute later, saying she had bad cell service but that she would see Cee-cee at Stacks in the morning.

She couldn't betray Anna's trust. Not now. Not with something so important. But hiding something like this from Cee-cee was a betrayal of another kind, and the duplicity was literally making Stephanie sick.

"Please let it be nothing so I can rip Anna a new one for putting us through this and we can all make a pact to never do something like this to each other in the future," she murmured softly, hands clasped.

Her thoughts were brought to a screeching halt as the sound of glass shattering broke the momentary quiet. She said a silent prayer for patience as she hurried out of the room and down the stairs toward the kitchen, where her father and Eva were.

She half expected to find one of them holding a head wound next to a just-launched vase while the other glowered with unchecked fury, but what she found was actually harder to take. Pop was standing at the kitchen island staring down at the shattered teacup on the floor, his face pale as Eva rubbed his arm in comfort.

"It's okay, Red. You're all right," she murmured, not even a hint of the anger or irritation from minutes before in her voice.

"Why is it doing that? Why is my hand shaking like that?"

Stephanie started to step into the room, but Eva caught her eye and shook her head almost imperceptibly.

For a second, Stephanie bristled. She was his daughter, after all. Surely she should see what was going on. When her father leaned into Eva, though, Stephanie faltered, stepping back into the hallway as Pop continued.

"I hate for the girls to see me like this. Weak and helpless. I don't want to be a burden. It's so damn humiliating."

"I know it, Red. They just want to help, though, and do what's best for you. And they can help you better if you stop barking at everyone and just tell them how you're feeling," Eva replied in a hushed tone as she pressed him into a chair and began to pick up the glass. "You're a tough old goat. It's a trait you've passed on to all three of those girls. They can handle it."

But that was where Eva had it wrong. Stephanie wasn't so sure she could handle it right now. As infuriating as she found his cantankerousness to be, it was infinitely better than bearing witness to his pain and shame.

She slunk back up the stairs wordlessly and then made her way back into her bedroom. Part of being strong was knowing how much pressure she could take before she cracked under the weight of it, and she was at a critical point. She desperately needed to disengage from all of this right now, before she shattered as surely as that teacup had.

She padded over to her dresser and reached into the top drawer to pull out a box of chocolates she'd received from the owner of one of her patients the week before. Her appetite had been nonexistent the past couple days and she'd skipped dinner, but she knew she needed to get something in her stomach. She also needed something to keep her busy until she was exhausted enough to fall asleep.

With that in mind, she crossed the room to the reading nook that had doubled as Paul's study, unwrapping the chocolates as she went.

A few months before, she'd taken on the task of cleaning his clothes out of their walk-in closet. She'd gotten derailed when she'd found that strange note in his sports jacket pocket, but she'd muscled through. It had been a big step, and she'd needed some time to psych herself up to go any further with the big purge. Now seemed like as good a time as any to continue.

She stiffened her shoulders as she stepped into the little room, realizing it was the first time since his funeral that she'd done so. Sure, she'd had to gather paperwork, and life insurance policies and the like, but after that? She'd avoided it like the plague.

As she sucked in a breath, she immediately remembered why.

His things were everywhere. His favorite sweater slung over the back of his chair. The dog-eared book he'd been reading. A note with a grocery list on it. *Apples, cheddar cheese*, and most achingly, *Steph's favorite tea*. But moreover, it smelled like him. Not like him, exactly. But like the space she associated with him. Leather and the worn paper of old books. It used to smell of that and lemon furniture polish, but she'd even stopped cleaning in there and dust lay in a thick layer over everything.

As if on cue, her nose twitched and she let out a sneeze.

"Well, that won't do at all," she murmured past the ache in her throat. She paused to pluck a chocolate from the box and stuffed it into her mouth before setting the rest on the chair, then pushed up her pajama sleeves.

Nothing like a project to keep the mind occupied.

She bustled out into the hallway and grabbed some cleaning supplies before digging in. A good ninety minutes later, Paul's study was finally tidied to her standards, and she'd climbed into bed wrapped in his sweater with an armload of old file folders and paperwork to sort and the book he'd never finished.

She popped another chocolate into her mouth, surprised to find she was feeling marginally better. As much as she hated throwing anything of his out, touching Paul's things, reading over passages of his favorite books, sitting where's he'd spent so many hours sitting himself, the supple leather worn to fit his body, had been its own type of comfort. She'd felt so alone the past couple days, and now she felt like he was there with her in some small way.

She huddled into the covers and let out a sigh of relief as she heard the front door click shut and the locks tumble.

That meant Pop was officially asleep and Eva had gone for the night. One good thing, typically once he was in bed, he didn't come out of his bedroom until morning, which meant a drama-free rest of the night for her. A respite she sorely needed.

She glanced at the paperwork and then at the book.

If she was being totally honest with herself, she'd admit that neither was exactly escapist fodder. Paul had been on a nonfiction kick the year he'd passed, and the hardcover book about the Civil War made the old pay stubs and bank statements look almost appealing.

Still, she finally settled on the book and laid it on her lap. She nudged the cover and the book fell open to page seventy-three, where a crisp-looking receipt marked the page. There were only a few items on it. A bacon, egg and cheese sandwich and a French toast platter plus two cups of coffee from a brunch restaurant by the pier called Pietro's. The bill total was a whopping fourteen bucks, plus a five dollar tip. Paul's mother had been a waitress and he'd always been a great tipper. Nothing interesting in the least. Certainly nothing that would have Stephanie's whole body trembling like she'd been doused in ice water.

No, it was the time and date stamp that had done that.

10:37AM, on the day Paul had died. Two hours after he'd supposedly been on his boat fishing.

Stephanie stared at the receipt in stunned silence, mind reeling.

She thought of her assumptions about a drama-free evening just moments before and let out a bubble of hysterical laughter through the veil of tears...

Oh, Paul, what did you do?

Chapter Eleven

Max shifted in her seat and frowned at the large windows overlooking Main Street. Business had been steady that morning, but then clouds blew in and a brisk wind kicked in shortly after noon, bringing sleet with it. The forecast said it wouldn't last long, and the temperature was supposed to stay warm enough to keep the streets from freezing, but it had definitely reduced her flow of customers to a slow trickle.

Maybe this had been a mistake.

After her chat with Aunt Anna, she'd been feeling much more hopeful, but every time she'd tried to pin her mother down to ask her about buying custom muffins for the shop, Cee-cee had been too busy to talk. With her own shop, Mick, and now that stupid cupcake challenge, Max might as well be working down in Portland. She rarely saw her mother, let alone spoke to her, even though their businesses were less than two blocks apart.

Max struggled to keep her disappointment at bay. She'd been lonely in Portland. Sure, she'd worked long hours and spent most of her time at the office, but she'd only had a few friends and they'd been work friends. The only time they'd associated outside of the office was the occasional Friday night drinks. She'd had a couple of dates—nothing serious—but her career had gotten in the way. Most people had no idea the long hours a corporate accountant put in at the office, if they wanted to get ahead that is, and Max had definitely wanted to get ahead. She'd drank from her father's workaholic fount, vowing to never be like her mother—a stay-at-home mom who had no life of her own. But over the past few years, Max had realized that while she may have given her all to her office, her office didn't give a flying fig about her. It all became glaringly obvious when she'd come down with the flu and all her boss cared about was when she was coming back to work. Those numbers weren't going to add themselves, so maybe Max could work on them at home? She was just lying around anyway. Who cared if she had a 104-degree fever?

She knew she was done after that, but the real question was what could she do? A position in another corporate office would be just like this one—a thankless job with long hours. During lunch breaks, she'd gone on interviews at several small accounting firms, but they'd all made her feel claustrophobic and one had made her stomach roil with the scent of sauerkraut clinging to the walls.

As she contemplated what to do, she started questioning *where* she could do it. She was still lonely and she hadn't put down any roots in Portland. Her heart lay in Bluebird Bay. So during short breaks at work, she started searching for real estate in her hometown. First it was houses and condos, but then an office space slipped into her search. She flipped past it, and then she stopped. What if *that* was her answer? What if she could start her own business? Be her own boss. Set her own hours.

Her searches then shifted to commercial real estate and she began browsing retail spaces. She still didn't know what she wanted to do—she was hoping inspiration would strike when she saw the perfect space. And it *had* struck when she saw the retail space on Main Street. As soon as she saw the photos with the brick walls and the hardwood floors, she instantly knew she wanted to open a bookstore in that very location. She loved to read and she loved the idea of puttering around a bookstore, so she'd taken a couple of days off and had driven back home to see the building, not telling anyone what she was doing. Not even her mother. At least not until she'd made a decision.

Max was elated the day her mother had called and asked her to dinner on the spur of the moment. She'd just quit her job and was in the process of packing up her apartment. Now was the perfect opportunity to let her mother in on her surprise as well as the slightly embarrassing part of her plan to ask her parents to let her temporarily move back home until she got the bookstore open. She knew her practical father would be furious with her decision, but her mother would understand and be supportive.

Celia hadn't let her down.

She had cheered Max on every step of the way, but she'd been dealing with her *own* life upheaval. Max's father had just left, and her mother was going through a season of discovery, and apparently, new love. Which meant her mother's time—which had been plentiful—was now tied up with her own life.

This was not what Max had expected. At all.

Since Max's earliest memories, Celia had always been there for her. Always watching over her and Gabe when they played outside. Volunteering as the team mom every season for soccer, softball, football, track, all from kindergarten to high school. Celia had held multiple elected positions in the PTA. Max could always count on her mother to step in wherever needed. Max's friends had been embarrassed by their moms, but not Max. Her mother was a stalwart in a storm and Max had always known she was lucky to have her.

So Max had to admit that she'd expected her mother to help more with the opening of the store, and although she'd never admit it out loud, she'd thought her mother might like volunteering in the bookstore. Mother and daughter working together every day. Max had been looking forward to so much one-on-one time with her mother. In Max's more introspective moments, she admitted it would have been nice to have the free help. She couldn't afford to hire anyone this early on, and her mother had always volunteered to help her so much in the past...

In Max's daydreams, that was the part she'd loved the most. Not the free labor, but spending endless hours with her mother milling around the shop. The two of them chatting and laughing and talking about books. The customers walking in and her mother greeting them. Helping them find the perfect book or gift. *Everyone*, including Max, loved being around Celia and Max knew she would have been a huge draw.

Max had been right, only Celia was drawing customers in with her own business.

In hindsight, Max knew she'd been wrong to make assumptions, but then her mother had always jumped in feet first, eager and willing to help Max make her dreams come true. Why would this be any different? Especially when Max was taking such a big risk.

The front door opened and she shifted her gaze to see Robbie saunter through the door, tiny ice pellets stuck to his thick, black hair. He wore all black—jeans, boots, coat, shirt.

It was like his uniform, and for all she knew, it was. It was just one of his quirks of being a metal sculptor, a profession she was still getting used to, along with the odd work hours and his insane sleep schedule.

But he was the quintessential brooding artist, and he was totally hot and sexy too. She'd been intrigued and flattered that he'd not only taken notice of her during a First Friday visit to his gallery, but then also asked her out for a drink when it was over.

Her mother had hated him the moment she'd laid eyes on him, not that she'd bothered to do much more than that. She was too busy with her own life. The life she was building without Max.

"Hey, babe," Robbie called out as he sauntered toward her.

She got up from her stool and walked around the counter, giving him a soft kiss when she reached him. "What are you doing out in this mess?"

"Checking on you. I figured you wouldn't have many customers, so we could hang out."

It also helped that his studio and gallery were a half block away, but she had to admit, the unnecessary comment about her lack of customers stung a little.

She put her hands on her hips. "You're still stuck on the McDermot project."

They hadn't been dating long, but she knew that Robbie worked on both personal projects and commissioned pieces. For the McDermot project, Robbie had been hired to create an ornamental sculpture marrying Maine seacoast wildlife with the sleek, contemporary McDermot house. Last she'd heard he still hadn't come up with a concept to present to them and he only had a couple of days left.

He unzipped his leather jacket and flopped down on the sofa. "Guilty as charged."

She'd never dated an artist before, and she struggled to understand the whole muse process. Accounting was black-and-white—the numbers added up or they didn't. There was no waiting for inspiration. What if inspiration never came?

He patted the seat next to her, then crooked his fingers in a *come here* gesture.

She shook her head. "The shop's still open. I don't want someone walking in and seeing me lounging around."

"It's nasty out there, Maxy. No one's coming in. You might as well hang up the closed sign. I did."

"Your gallery is open whenever you see fit to open it," she countered.

"That's not true. It's open on Fridays and Saturdays."

That was because he had hired help to man it, but she didn't feel like arguing the point.

He gave her a sexy grin. "Besides, haven't you ever wanted to do it in your store? We've definitely christened my studio and gallery. It's your turn."

Her face flushed. Honestly, she'd never considered it. Robbie's studio was also his apartment...and the gallery could be blamed on too much to drink. She was definitely sober now. "Behind a bookstack?"

His grin spread. "Sure. If that's what you're into."

There was no denying that Robbie had a healthy libido and when he got bored or stuck on a project, he claimed sex helped jog things loose. While she hadn't minded being his muse, she didn't want to blur the lines between her sexual escapades and her own business space.

"Not right now," she said, self-consciously looking down and smoothing her skirt. "I was working on inventory," she lied, not liking herself very much for doing so. What happened to the strong independent woman she'd been in Portland? But she knew that Robbie sometimes got pouty when she turned him down, and she didn't want to deal with his mood.

Deep down she knew that was a warning sign that this relationship was doomed, but she batted it away. It wasn't like they were serious. Robbie was a fling—a very sexually fulfilling fling—and nothing else. But then, she knew that wasn't quite true either. She was desperately lonely and Robbie helped fill that void in her heart. Sure, he didn't really fit the empty space, but like Aunt Anna said, she was young. She could have her fun.

She could let him distract her from the pain of feeling like she'd lost her mother, the failure of her store, and the mind-numbing loneliness that had started to send her into a depression. Sure, Robbie wasn't the right guy for her, but he was helping her, even if he didn't know it. Soon the relationship would run its course, and he'd move on to the next woman he claimed inspired him.

And then she'd be alone again.

Robbie got up and slowly advanced toward her, like a predator stalking his prey, and she could feel her resolve melting. Sex with him was a distraction for her too.

"We're not going to make a habit of this," she said in as strict a tone as she could muster.

Promises filled his eyes and she took a step toward the front door.

"Where are you going?" he asked in a low growl.

"To lock the front door."

He slowly shook his head. "Don't you think there's a certain thrill to the risk of being caught?"

Max sucked in her breath. "No, Robbie! This is my business!"

He closed the distance between them and buried his face into the crook of her neck. "Okay, little Maxy." His breath sent a fire through her veins. "If you say so."

Anger blossomed and part of her wanted to tell him off for being so lackadaisical about her business, the business he knew she was struggling to keep afloat. All she needed was for someone to walk in and see them fornicating and then everyone would stay away—or show up hoping to catch her in the act. Neither option was good.

She stood stiff and erect, weighing her options. There was a time her anger might have sent him packing with a warning not to let the door hit him where the good Lord split him. But her roommate was out of town again—not that she was around much anymore anyway. If she told Robbie off, he'd go back to his studio and pout, and she'd be left alone. Again. Hours and hours of emptiness and loneliness. The thoughts of her failure condemning her. Second-guessing her decisions. Her anxiety sky-rocketing. A now-familiar pressure on her chest intensified, making her feel like she was going to be suffocated, her life feeling like it was spiraling out of control.

No, she couldn't risk upsetting him. She'd lock the door and he'd be fine with it, especially if she encouraged him to head to the back room.

She was desperate for some kind of human connection.

Even if it was with Robbie.

Chapter Twelve

Cee-cee felt off when she pulled into the Stacks parking lot Friday morning. She chided herself, aware she was being pulled in too many directions. She'd gotten up earlier than usual to do the morning baking so she could meet her sisters for breakfast. It had seemed like an easy and practical solution, but then she'd nearly screwed up a batch of Ho-Ho-Honey and Buttermilk sponge cupcakes with a cinnamon praline buttercream because she was so preoccupied with the upcoming competition. As a newcomer to the baking world, she felt like she had to go above and beyond to prove that she deserved to be in the competition. So she and Mick had streamed a bunch of televised baking contests, writing down things to try and avoid, and she had to admit the stress was getting to her. Not like that would stop her from meeting her sisters this morning, though Steph had been weird on the phone the day before, and Cee-cee's sister intuition had set off warning bells.

Something was up.

There was no denying she'd stretched herself to the limit, but as she climbed out of the car, Cee-cee could think of little else beside her sister, and worried about what could have Stephanie on edge. Was it Pop? No doubt Steph was taking the full brunt of dealing with him, making Cee-cee feel guilty. She'd dealt with Pop for several years now, mostly on her own, but she had to admit that he hadn't lived with her and that his mind and attitude had significantly worsened since the fire. Deep down she knew that he wouldn't be going back to his home once it was finished, but she couldn't bring herself to consider residential care. It would kill him.

Stephanie and Anna were already seated when she walked into the restaurant. She took a seat and noticed that they were unusually quiet and tense. Were they fighting again? They bickered more than a couple of fishmongers' wives.

"Your face is looking better, Anna," Cee-cee said as she reached for the carafe of coffee and poured some into her cup.

Anna absently lifted her hand to her cheek. "Oh," she said as though just remembering her face had been bruised. "Yeah." Then she wrapped her hands around her coffee mug and focused on the beverage inside.

That response was so un-Anna-like that the hairs on the back of Cee-cee's neck stood on end. Then she remembered that she'd meant to call Anna, but the week had gotten away from her.

"Anna," Cee-cee said with forced brightness. "I'm so sorry I haven't called you back yet. Life's just been so crazy. Can you tell me about that cupcake flavor now?"

Anna's gaze lifted and she blinked, a smile that looked plastered on spreading across her face. "Oh, yeah. While I was in Alaska, one of the researchers made the most delicious pancakes. I thought it might be a great cupcake flavor idea."

Cee-cee leaned forward. "Oh? I'm all ears. Mick and I are coming up with as many different unique flavors as possible so I'll be able to pull from our list depending on the challenge."

"Well," Anna said, warming to the conversation. "Brynn made these amazing pecan pancakes. When slathered with butter and real maple syrup...let's just say some of us gained a few pounds. I can only imagine how phenomenal they'd be if she'd cooked them in bacon fat like she was thinking of trying next time around." She patted her tummy and grinned.

"That's awesome," Cee-cee said, grabbing her phone and pulling up her note app. "I'll definitely give them a few test runs." Then, without giving it a thought, she added, "Maybe you'd like to come help me bake a batch or two." She shot a glance to Steph. "All three of us. It will be fun." But even as the words fell out, she wondered when she'd fit it in. If history were any indicator, baking with her sisters would probably result in more wine consumption and laughing than cupcake-making.

"Yeah," Stephanie said. "Sounds fun."

The waitress walked over with her notepad and more energy than a person had a right to have this early. "What can I get you ladies?"

Cee-cee hadn't had time to look at the menu, but she'd been here enough to know what she wanted—a veggie omelet. Steph ordered her usual Belgian waffle with mixed berry compote, but Anna only ordered a biscuit and bacon.

"Are you feeling okay?" Cee-cee asked with a frown as the waitress took the menus away.

Anna's eyes widened. "What? Why do you ask?"

Something weird was definitely going on. "You're not yourself today and I've never seen you pass up the pancake platter here."

Anna looked like she was standing in front of a firing squad.

Stephanie leaned forward. "Before you showed up, Anna mentioned that her stomach wasn't quite right, but she didn't want to cancel."

Stephanie had always been a terrible liar and this time was no different, but Cee-cee bit her tongue. She couldn't help feeling hurt. Something was going on and Stephanie was clearly in on it.

They'd left her out.

Were they punishing her for setting boundaries and putting her own needs first?

Stephanie tried to make small talk, telling Cee-cee about the two yoga classes she'd taught that week.

"I really love it," Stephanie said, her eyes bright with excitement. "I'm so glad I decided to step out of my comfort zone." She hesitated, and gave Cee-cee a soft smile. "You're the one who inspired me to go for it."

Cee-cee sat back in surprise. "Me?"

"Yeah," Steph said. "Look at you. Your life was turned upside down. You could have wallowed, but you grabbed the bull by the horns and decided to turn lemons into lemonade."

Cee-cee didn't know what to say. "Steph…"

"So I'm a lot slower than you, but I'm getting there."

"Losing a beloved husband to an untimely death is a far cry from a disinterested spouse leaving you for another woman."

"A loss is a loss, Cee-cee," Stephanie said quietly. "And you've handled it with grace and poise. I'm happy you've found happiness with your new career and with Mick. You couldn't have found a greater guy."

"So you're not mad at me?" Cee-cee asked, bursting with love for her sister.

Steph's mouth dropped open. "Why would you think I was mad at you?"

"You and Anna are both acting so strangely."

Stephanie cast a long glance to Anna then finally back to Cee-cee. "Anna's not feeling quite right."

"Is it your injuries?" Cee-cee asked. "Have you overdone it?"

"No," Anna said, and Cee-cee realized how uncharacteristically quiet she was. "I'm just out of sorts."

Stephanie's forehead wrinkled, a look Cee-cee recognized as irritation.

What in the world was going on?

"Speaking of moving forward," Stephanie said, "I'm still going through Paul's things and throwing some stuff out, but I found something...odd."

That seemed to perk Anna up. "What?"

"A receipt from the morning that Paul died."

"Wait," Cee-cee said. "I thought Paul left the house to go fishing and never came home?"

"That's what I thought too," Steph said, her voice tight. "But the receipt was for a breakfast for two at Pietro's."

"Was he meeting someone?" Cee-cee asked. "A business associate?"

"Maybe...," she said. "But we spoke that morning. In fact, he tried to get me to play hooky and go fishing with him and made no mention of a breakfast plan with anyone. He always told me before."

"Surely you don't think he was having an affair," Anna said, some of her feistiness returning. "Because that man loved you like no man has ever loved a woman before." She shot a grimace to Cee-cee. "No offense to Mick."

"None taken," she said, relieved Anna was acting more like herself.

"I don't know what it means," Steph said. "It's probably nothing. But it doesn't matter because we'll never know." She forced a smile. "You must be excited about Gabe and Sasha's wedding. Have they decided where to have it yet?"

Cee-cee could take a hint, not that she blamed her sister for changing the subject. No one had ever doubted that Paul loved Stephanie, but terrible things must have been going through her head.

The waitress brought their food and they dug in.

"I hear Max has a new boyfriend," Steph said. "That artist that took over the gallery on Main Street?"

Cee-cee made a face. "He's not her usual boyfriend, so I'm hoping it blows over soon. Especially since I've heard he goes through women faster than rabbits breed. I can't believe she's letting herself settle for him."

"Can you even hear yourself?" Anna snapped. "You sound like Pop."

Cee-cee stared at her in disbelief. "*What?*"

"Have you even bothered to get to know him?"

Taken aback, Cee-cee said, "Well, we met, but I didn't spend a lot of time talking to him, no…"

"Of course you haven't," Anna retorted. "You're too busy living your own life and you don't have time for anyone else. Not even your own daughter."

"I knew you were mad at me for not calling you!" Cee-cee countered, pointing her fork at her sister.

"Are you *serious*?" Anna asked, shaking her head in disgust. "I'm talking about your *daughter*, Celia. The one who has a failing business and a boyfriend you won't even take the time to get to know."

Cee-cee's anger faded. She had to admit that Anna was right, but there was something else going on here. Anna had a wild, desperate look in her eyes, like she was about ready to explode with anxiety and her outburst was a valve letting off steam.

She was about to pin her down and get to the bottom it when Anna's phone rang. Fear and apprehension filled both of her sisters' faces. Then Anna sprang into action, rifling through her purse and becoming more frantic when she hadn't found it by the third ring.

"What's going on?" Cee-cee demanded.

Both sisters ignored her. Then Anna pulled out the phone and fumbled to answer it. "Hello?"

Stephanie looked terrified as she watched Anna listen to whoever was on the other side.

"Are you sure?" Anna asked as the color faded from her face.

Stephanie sucked in a breath.

Cee-cee could have cut the tension with a butter knife, and she wanted to shake the both of them and insist they tell her what was going on, but she didn't. Mostly because she was terrified of what they were going to tell her.

"This afternoon? Okay," Anna said, seeming to shrink before Cee-cee's eyes. She ended the call and set her phone on the table.

"Anna," Stephanie said. "What did they say?"

Anna turned to look at her with a blank expression on her face.

"What's going on?" Cee-cee asked again, but her sisters still ignored her.

Anna's eyes filled with tears, and Steph grabbed her sister's hand and squeezed. "It's going to be okay, Anna. We'll get through this."

Anna nodded.

Cee-cee watched her sisters in horror.

"Now what did they say?" Steph asked, sounding more terse.

"They think it's cancer, but I need to go to see the oncology surgeon to have a biopsy," Anna said. "Dr. Waverly already called him and he had a cancellation, so I'm supposed to see him this afternoon."

"Cancer?" Cee-cee forced past a lump in her throat.

Stephanie turned to Cee-cee, clearly in take-charge mode. "We'll fill you in about everything in a minute." Then she gave Anna her full attention. "Okay. I'm clearing my schedule for the day and going with you. We'll handle this together."

Cee-cee wasn't sure how long Anna had known about this, but Stephanie was definitely in the loop. The two of them had known that Anna might have cancer and hadn't included her in their inner circle.

Why?

She swallowed the pain and hurt feelings, telling herself now wasn't the time to demand answers. Her baby sister likely had cancer, and she needed Cee-cee's love and support, not her whiney questions and accusations.

"I'm clearing my schedule too. I'm coming."

Anna gave her a wary stare. "You don't even know what's going on."

"I've heard enough to understand that you need your sisters. Both of us."

"But your cupcake shop...," Anna stammered. "Your competition."

"You're more important than the shop or a stupid competition," Cee-cee said. "Any day of the week."

Anna may not have included her before her diagnosis, but Cee-cee was going to be part of it now. It was time to go into sister mode.

Chapter Thirteen

For Anna, the next handful of days ran together like a watercolor study in black and gray. A dreamlike landscape of doctor visits and needles and scalpels and conversations her brain had largely blocked from her mind in some sort of intrinsic protective response that she wished she could bottle. At the end of it, Anna found herself back in her apartment, flanked by her sisters. The biopsy had been marginally uncomfortable. But the wait for her results? Was the keenest, most excruciating pain she'd ever felt, and she'd do just about anything to make it end.

"The mulligatawny is ready. You hungry?"

Anna looked up to find Cee-cee standing over her, the worry line between her eyes seeming etched in since they'd left Stacks after that fateful call. Thank God for her. And Stephanie, too. Anna wouldn't have been able to get through this without them. Cee-cee had stood by her side for the biopsy and left poor Mick in charge of the shop for the rest of the day. After Anna had gone to bed, she'd snuck away and stayed up all night, baking like a madwoman for the weekend, before rushing back to Anna's, leaving Pete the high school kid and Mick in control again. And Steph had been just as supportive, closing her practice for the weekend, leaving just a phone number for emergencies. She'd even gotten Eva to stay with Pop as they rallied around Anna and kept her busy with old movies and board games.

As she met her oldest sister's haunted gaze, Anna forced a smile. "I'd love some." As Cee-cee turned to get her soup, Anna stopped her with a hand on her arm. "You're the best, Cee-cee. And I love you so much."

Cee-cee's eyes went suspiciously shiny as she cleared her throat. "You too, kiddo," she murmured before she pulled away and scurried into the kitchen.

Anna got it. They were all walking around like frayed wires, crackling with terror, emotions so close to the surface that everything felt like an open wound. She didn't want to make either of her sisters even more emotional, but they needed to know how much she appreciated them being there for her like this. Anna and Steph had their ups and downs before the fateful trip to Alaska—Anna had been so focused on her career and hadn't realized that she needed to be more present for their dad, and Steph had been having her own struggles with Pop. And then, Anna had been so hard on Cee-cee for not making the time for her and even coming down on her over Max. But when the chips were down...when it really counted, they'd been there for her.

They always were.

It was one of the things about coming home that she never had when she was away. Family. Community. Unconditional love and support. In times like this, it was priceless. In her rare moments of clarity over the past couple of days, she felt humbled by it.

But mostly? She just felt terrified.

"Here you go, sweetie," Steph said as she padded into the room and handed her a steaming soup mug and a spoon.

Anna thanked her and took a moment to study her sister's face. Unlike Cee-cee who wore her emotions on her sleeve, Steph was much more stoic. Her training made her an absolute gem during a crisis. She always managed to compartmentalize and get the job done. Just the matter of fact way she processed information and set a course to deal with every hurdle as it came was a comfort in itself. But it came at a price, and Anna could see her iron will was flagging. Dark bruise-like shadows marred the hollows beneath Steph's eyes, her skin was pale, and her cheeks looked just a bit more hollow than they had the week before. If she'd had the strength, Anna would've rushed into her room to grab her camera and snap a picture of her. She'd call it *A Crack in the Shield*.

She tore her gaze away and spooned up some soup, breathing in the comforting smell before taking a bite.

"Perfect," she murmured with a sigh.

Steph managed a smile. "I'll give your compliments to the chef."

"What's she doing in there?" Anna asked, the banging of pots and pans echoing through the walls.

"I can't say for sure, but I think she's reorganizing all your crap. I left when I heard her muttering about only lunatics putting their steak knives in the same slot as their butter knives."

That got a genuine grin out of Anna, which had Steph responding in kind. Then Anna's phone rang.

The two of them locked gazes and the banging stopped. Anna swallowed hard and set down her mug as she leaned forward and peered down at the screen.

Dr. Epstein, the surgical oncologist.

Her hand trembled as she pressed the speaker button. "Hello?"

"Can I speak to Anna Sullivan, please?" Dr. Epstein said, his tone warm and even.

No clues there. She tried to control the tremor in her voice as Cee-cee stepped into the room, eyes wide, nostrils flaring in barely restrained panic.

"Yes, this is Anna."

"Hi there. I'm calling to let you know that we've received the results back from the biopsy. If you can, I'd like you to come in so we can discuss—"

"Just tell me," she whispered. She would never forget this moment. Hanging there, on the precipice. Knowing the truth already, in the deepest part of herself, but still harboring that infernal, pathetic ember of hope burning somewhere inside her that just maybe this was all a bad dream. "Just tell me now, doctor. Both my sisters are here, I'm not alone…I just can't wait another moment."

A beat of silence.

"It's cancer. I know that's not the news you want to hear, and it's certainly not the news I wanted to deliver, but it is what we suspected. The good news is that it's treatable."

Words, words, words. Something about a lumpectomy, and radiation, and family history. Something else about margins and staging and recovery time, followed by assurances and positivity. But Anna could process none of it, beyond the single word.

Cancer.

Images rushed through her mind like a collage. Their mother, fading away before their very eyes, the life slowly draining from her like she was being sucked dry by an invisible, insatiable vampire who fed on vitality. Standing by her bedside, squeezing eye drops into her half-open eyes because she was too weak to blink. Smoothing balm onto her cracked lips when her body was nothing but a dried-up husk after they'd removed her feeding tube and IVs.

It was Steph who eventually said goodbye to the doctor and disconnected the call. And it was Steph who snapped Anna out of what was surely some level of shock.

"Don't fall apart on us now, kiddo. I know it doesn't seem like it right now, but this is all good news. It's early days, not like with Mom, okay?" she murmured as she knelt before Anna and rubbed her arms in brisk strokes like she was trying to stave off frostbite.

"Sh-she's right," Cee-cee was saying. "The word shook me for a second, but once the doctor started talking I knew it was going to be okay. Did you hear what he said?" She perched on the armrest of the couch and rubbed Anna's back in slow circles. "Based on the biopsy, they should be able to go in, remove all the cancer cells and hit it with some radiation. No chemo, no major surgery. You'll be in the hospital one day."

Anna sucked in a shuddering breath and nodded, trying to find a corner of her brain that could still conjure a rational thought. She recalled just a week before, when she'd cried about a gray hair, and hot flashes, and a couple of bruises. When she'd fought with her sister over a missed phone call. When airheaded witch Maryanne Brown had the power to ruin her mood.

It seemed like a million years ago, now. So silly. So inconsequential. Because now she had cancer.

The diagnosis was no surprise. She'd known from the first visit with Dr. Waverly, the second her fingers frozen in place and she'd asked Anna about her last mammogram. What was surprising is just how devastating hearing it out loud was. And that was okay. She had the right to feel devastated and afraid and confused and—yeah—a little cheated that she'd drawn one of the short straws. But letting herself dive into those feelings was a slippery slope. One that could result in something far worse than a few broken ribs and bruises. She had to try to pull herself out of this nosedive or she would do herself more harm than good.

"Okay," she murmured as she sat up, only just now realizing that she'd been slumped forward with her head between her legs. "Okay, I'm okay," she repeated, nodding vigorously to prove it. "We got this, right?"

"We so totally got this," Cee-cee parroted.

"We absolutely do," Steph added firmly.

"When?" Anna asked, shooting a glance at Steph, who was surely taking mental notes as the doctor had droned on with details.

"Sooner the better. Tentatively, Friday, but he wanted to give you some time to let the news sink in. His scheduling person will call back before five and firm things up."

"If you can do Friday, that would be great. You'd probably be feeling well enough to enjoy the rest of the holidays."

"Exactly," Steph agreed. "Based on the biopsy, they won't be taking a huge amount of tissue, so you'll be uncomfortable but you'll get to the other side of it in just a couple weeks."

Based on the biopsy.

That was the scary part. What would they find when they went in to remove the lump? Would it be as cut and dried as the doctor and her sisters hoped?

"But Mom . . ."

"You can't compare yourself to Mom. She was more than a quarter of a century older than you are right now and had a weaker constitution in general. Things had also progressed much further, she had lots of symptoms that she ignored, and she wasn't nearly as fit and healthy as you are," Cee-cee argued.

"Cee-cee's right," Steph piped in. "I loved Mom to pieces but she wasn't diligent about her health and waited far too long to tell anyone she was having problems. I don't blame her for that. The time she grew up in prized that grin and bear it mentality. But she had lots of signs that, had she told us about them, could've saved her life. I regret that so much...not asking her more about things like that..."

The three of them sat in silence, lost in their own reflections and regrets for long moments until Steph slapped her thighs and stood.

"We're going to fight this. And you're going to beat it. I won't have it any other way."

Please, God, let her be right.

There was only one way to find out. And suddenly, the surgery couldn't come soon enough.

"Let's call the doctor's office back and confirm. Friday it is," Anna said with a note of finality.

She reached for her soup and shoveled a bite into her mouth as her mind began to churn. She was in the midst of a war. There was an invader in her body. An unwelcome intruder, intent on doing her harm.

And she wanted it the hell out.

Chapter Fourteen

Stephanie had heard the phrase "put through the wringer" before. But after losing her mother, her husband, and nearly losing her father this past summer, she'd never known it quite as keenly as she had this past few days. Those events had been devastating. Hell, some days, they still were. But her husband's death had come out of nowhere. A total shock. The fire at Pop's had been a brief flash of terror followed by intense relief. And, as terrible as watching her mother die had been—for her more than anyone, as they'd always been so close—it was nothing like spending an interminable week contemplating the possibility of losing her baby sister.

Anna wasn't out of the woods yet. They still had the surgery to get through and there would always be that niggling worry of a reoccurrence, even if everything went perfectly smoothly. But all things considered, her relief was like a living, breathing entity. Anna was still scared, they all were. The worst of it was likely behind them, though, and it felt a little like they'd cheated death.

Which was fair. Death owed Stephanie one.

A big one.

She settled back into her desk chair and popped a mint into her mouth as she went over her schedule for the day. She was just about to pour herself a second cup of coffee when the office phone rang.

"Dr. Ketterman," she murmured, pressing a hand to her achy lower back. Anna's apartment only had one bedroom, and she and Cee-cee had taken turns sharing a bed with Anna while the other took the pull-out couch, which had been slightly less comfortable than sleeping on a pile of tap shoes wrapped in a potato sack.

"Hey, Mom."

She grinned reflexively at the sound of Todd's voice. Talking with her oldest son never failed to cheer her up. Her smile faded as she realized she still wasn't supposed to talk about Anna's condition. She'd felt bad enough keeping it from Cee-cee before they'd known the diagnosis. Her oldest sister had been gracious enough not to mention the deception as the gravity of Anna's situation had unfolded, but Stephanie had seen the hurt and confusion in her eyes when she'd put it all together at their pancake breakfast. The last thing she wanted to do was drive a wedge between her and Todd. Still, this wasn't her secret to tell. If Anna wanted to keep it close to the vest until...well, the end of time, frankly, Stephanie would respect that.

"So good to hear your voice, sweetie. How have you been?" She held the phone to her ear, navigating the cord as she made her way to the coffee pot.

"I'm good. Nothing big here, just calling to check on you and Shelley and wanted to see if we had firmed up plans for Christmas Eve yet."

In past years, Steph handled Thanksgiving, Cee-cee and Nate had hosted Christmas Eve, and the families each did their own thing on Christmas Day, with Anna bouncing from house to house depending on her mood. Now that Cee-cee had sold the beach house and moved into a small apartment above the cupcake shop, they'd all been trying to figure out where to get together. Stephanie had considered hosting both, but Christmas had been the toughest holiday since Paul's death. She had to be honest and kind to herself by admitting she couldn't handle it. Not just the physical work of it all, but the emotional weight. And that was before the usual family sniping and petty arguments ratcheted things up a notch. If they celebrated elsewhere, it was a finite event that would start when she walked in the door and ended when she walked out, which could be as early as she wanted. In the end, she'd decided to stick to her guns and not offer up her place.

Her own kids and Max were in the same boat as Cee-cee, with small apartments or houses that didn't work for entertaining more than a few people at a time. Sasha, Gabe's fiancé, had offered to host, but they were still in the middle of renovating their cottage. Despite assuring them the work would be done well before Christmas, the contractors had seemed to disappear around Thanksgiving and work still hadn't resumed. It wasn't looking good on that front, and who knew where Anna would be, both physically and emotionally?

Steph poured her coffee and took a second to mull that over before replying. "You know what? Let's go out."

Her suggestion was met with silence, but she pushed forward, quickly warming to the idea.

"The Pelican has an amazing Christmas Eve buffet everyone raves about. Last year, Jackie went and said they had everything from ham and turkey and all the fixings to a huge seafood bar. Sticky toffee pudding and black forest cake for dessert. Better than anything I could manage, I'm sure. And it will be my treat. What do you say?"

Dinner for more than a dozen of them wouldn't be cheap, but her practice was doing better than ever. Besides, it would be worth every penny to have all the worry about it off her mind. She was sure her sisters would feel the same. One less thing to think about during a difficult time. She already felt better just thinking about it.

"I'm game. I'm not sure Pop will be too thrilled. You know how he feels about tradition," Todd said.

"Pop will have to get over it. Not everything is about him. Especially right now."

She took a sip of her black coffee, not realizing what she'd said until the phone went silent again.

"What do you mean, 'right now'?" he asked carefully.

Crap.

"I-I just mean with Aunt Cee-cee busy with her competition and Aunt Anna all banged up and such. This will make it easy for everyone."

"Okay, if you're sure that's all…"

The door of her office jangled open and she nearly wept with gratitude as Beckett stepped in with a smile of greeting.

"I'm sure. Look, honey, someone just walked into the clinic, so I've got to go. I'll talk to you in the next few days to firm up the Christmas Eve plans, once I talk to my sisters. Love you."

"Love you too."

She could tell by his dubious tone he wasn't totally convinced, but he wasn't one to dwell, and he'd forget about it as soon as something else caught his attention. She was just grateful she didn't have to continue the charade any longer, because she was getting tired from all the tap dancing. She made a mental note to ask Anna what her plans were as far as telling the rest of the family and then turned her attention to welcome her visitor.

"Hey there!" she said warmly, setting her mug down. "How about a cup of coffee to warm you up?"

"Just had two at the diner before I came, thanks. I just wanted to check on Shelley. It's been a few weeks since I've seen him."

Sweet, sweet man. And a handsome one, to boot. She wondered idly if he and Anna had spoken again since their disastrous date. Anna had been preoccupied enough that it hadn't come up, and she wasn't about to ask Beckett. They were very friendly, but they didn't talk about their personal lives much.

"He looked excellent when I checked him before I opened for the day. I'm about to go give him his breakfast, if you'd like to join me."

She led him into what had been a large storage space in the back and had been converted into a mini-habitat for her favorite turtle.

"Wow, new pool?" Beckett asked with a low whistle. "That thing is huge."

For the first few months while Shelley was healing, Stephanie had kept him in a plastic kiddie pool. It was best for him not to move around much in any case, with all the stitched lacerations and the polyurethane covering his cracked shell still not completely cured. Once he'd largely healed, though, the pool hadn't been enough space for the large animal. She was still kicking around the idea of bringing him to the aquarium, but hadn't had the chance to really research that idea thoroughly with everything that had been going on.

"One of my patients actually brought me that. He's a landscape artist, and the pool had been a water feature in one of his client's yards. They wanted to get rid of it, so he was about to trash it but then thought of Shelley. He dug it out, plugged in the holes where the fountains had fed through, and then brought it over. I'm thinking I might actually keep it even once Shelley is gone. I can't tell you the times it would've come in handy rehabilitating sea birds and the occasional otter."

She padded over to the cooler she kept in the corner filled with seaweed and mussels, Shelley's two favorite foods.

"I think it's great. Much more room. I called the aquarium yesterday and spoke to the director there about him," Beckett said, taking the pile of seaweed she handed him and lowering it into the pool until Shelley came paddling over. "He told me that, although they do have some programs that allow for rehab and release, if Shelley was given into their care, they wouldn't release him into the wild again. They don't have the staff or transportation to move him and whatnot."

She'd wondered about that, and part of her was relieved because it made her decision a lot easier. Shelley would stay here with her until Spring, then she would release him into the waters he called home. Part of her felt guilty, because although the pool was larger, it wasn't even close to large enough.

"We have to think long term, and I think it's best if he stays here until we can set him free into the wild," she said, watching fondly as Shelley munched on his breakfast.

"That sounds good to me. Let me know whenever you're ready, and we'll fire up the flatbed." He paused and then shot her a quick glance. "How's Anna doing? I haven't seen her since the adoption event."

Stephanie was careful to keep her expression neutral.

"She's lying low, being gentle with herself right now. I think the fall shook her up. She wasn't herself for a bit there."

Beckett nodded, his cheeks going ruddy. "I had wondered if it was something like that. We had dinner that night and she seemed...off. Like something was bothering her, but I didn't want to pry and she didn't seem inclined to share. I've been wanting to call her, but things ended so abruptly, I thought I should wait and see if she called me."

Interesting. Beckett's take on the date was a bit different than her sister's had been, and he clearly wasn't as turned off by her strange behavior as she'd assumed.

Stephanie tucked that knowledge away to tell Anna when the time was right, and smiled at Beckett.

"I know she thinks you're a great guy and she had a lot of fun, so maybe shoot her a text and check in at some point. She's definitely going through some life changes, but I'm sure she'd like to hear from you."

"Will do," he said, visibly relieved.

They chatted for a few more minutes before he took his leave and Stephanie headed back into her office to go over her schedule for the coming few weeks. She didn't want to schedule off more time than necessary, but it was imperative that she ensure anything major was taken care of leading up to Anna's surgery so that she had plenty of time off if need be. She had just made her last call for rescheduling when her cell phone rang.

Eva.

"Oh, Lord."

Eva typically didn't call unless Pop was being exceptionally difficult, so she braced herself as she answered.

"Hi Eva, everything okay?"

Everything wasn't okay. Eva's sister had been in a car accident. She was stable, but she'd broken her hip and needed Eva to fly down to New York to care for her.

Stephanie's stomach dropped and she leaned forward, pressing her head against her desk.

"I'm so sorry to hear that, Eva. I'm so glad she's not critically hurt. When will you be leaving?"

"Day after tomorrow when she gets released from the hospital. I know this puts you in a terrible spot, because I don't know when I'll be back..." Eva broke off and then continued in a rush. "I'm so sorry, doll. I wish I knew what else to do..."

"Family is family," Steph replied. "You take care of your sister and I'll worry about Pop."

They hammered out a few details for the next couple days and then disconnected.

Stephanie spared a glance at the clock on the wall. Forty minutes until her next appointment. Plenty of time for a total nervous breakdown.

Dear Lord, when it rained, it poured...

Chapter Fifteen

Anna loved her sisters to death—especially after they'd dropped everything to stay with her and offer their support while she waited to find out her diagnosis. Her reaction upon hearing she might have cancer had surprised her. Anna prided herself on being strong and brave. She'd camped in African deserts. She'd stared down a mountain lion. She'd lived in the Arctic for more than two months. But hearing that she might possibly have cancer—the very disease that had taken their mother—had brought her to her knees. She'd fallen to pieces and she didn't even want to think about what she would have done if her sisters hadn't been there to catch her.

But the moment Anna had received the confirmation, something in her changed. No longer living in limbo and armed with a plan of action laid out by her stellar medical team, Anna's confidence had returned and she felt like she could now face this head-on. She still needed her sisters, but she didn't need them *quite* so close. At least not the night before her surgery.

So she sent them home, and breathed a sigh of relief to have the empty apartment to herself. She'd had someone with her twenty-four seven for a week, and she was in need of some alone time. The worry was still there, especially her pre-surgery nerves, but the independent part of her needed to spend this night by herself.

The silence, however, left Anna alone with her thoughts. She may have a game plan, but she was still dealing with what-ifs. What if the cancer had metastasized? What if she ended up with a double mastectomy like her mother had? What if she was dead within three years of her diagnosis too?

"This is ridiculous," she muttered to herself. "I can what-if all day long, but I need to stick to the cold hard facts." Based on all the tests and scans, every medical professional involved thought she had a greater likelihood of catching it in time versus it spreading elsewhere. She needed to focus on the positive. It was much more her style.

What she needed was to keep her mind occupied and a book or a TV show wasn't going to cut it, so she turned to the one thing she often lost herself in—her work. She had just booted up her laptop to edit some photos from her Alaska trip when her phone rang. She almost let it go to voicemail without checking to see who was calling, but changed her mind. Steph or Cee-cee would worry if she didn't answer, and after everything they had done for her this week, she couldn't let that happen. But it was Max's name on the screen, so Anna answered right away. Her niece had been on her mind lately.

"Hey, sweet girl," Anna said in a chipper tone. "What's up with you?"

Max was silent for a moment as though she wasn't sure how to answer the question, then said, "Aunt Anna, would you mind if I came over to hang out tonight? I can even bring dinner."

Anna had enough leftovers from her sisters' many meals to last her into the next week, and she was looking forward to her alone time, but she could tell Max needed to see her. Something in her voice sounded off. "Sounds great," she said enthusiastically. "I was editing photos from my trip, but I'd much rather see you. Come on over."

"See you in about a half hour," Max said, sounding relieved before she disconnected.

Anna was about to set her phone down, but she noticed a missed text from Beckett that had been sent less than an hour before.

Beckett? Dear heavens. What could *he* be texting about? Her face heated with embarrassment thinking about her odd and awkward behavior at their dinner. She expected him to duck his head and run the other direction the next time she saw him in town. Relief swamped her when she read his message.

I hope you're feeling better now that you've had time to heal, and I was wondering if you'd like to go out to dinner again sometime.

Her first thought was that she hadn't had her surgery yet and how had he found out? Then she realized he was talking about her injuries from the fall in Alaska. Funny how they'd been so front and center in her life two weeks ago and now they were an afterthought. But his message suggested that he'd thought her odd behavior had been because of her injuries and not her own social ineptitude. God bless that man.

The real question was whether she wanted to go out with him again. He was a grandfather, for heaven's sake. *A grandfather.* But she had to admit that he was a pretty sexy grandfather, and a really nice guy to boot. Anna was old enough to be a grandmother herself, albeit a young one, and it was time to stop pretending she was still thirty-five. This health scare had taught her that life was short and she needed to live it. She needed family *and* friends.

I'd like that, but I'm busy through this weekend. Can we touch base next week?

He answered right away. *Can't wait for next week.*

Anna smiled to herself. Tomorrow she was having a surgery to have her breast cancer removed, and next week she was scheduling a date with Beckett Wright. This was life—messy and unplanned. And when she wasn't facing her own mortality—something she was dealing with on both counts—she embraced it wholeheartedly. She needed to embrace this too.

But right now she needed a shower, or Max might go running the other direction once she caught a whiff of her.

Anna had just gotten out of the shower and put on a pair of jammies when the doorbell rang. Max was at the door, holding up a paper bag with a Gino's Italian Restaurant logo on the front.

"I got your favorite," Max said with a grin.

"The five-cheese lasagna?" Anna asked hopefully.

"Please," Max groaned playfully. "You think I'm an amateur? It's the one and only."

"Then what are you doing out in the hall?" Anna asked, reaching for her arm and dragging her over the threshold. "Get in here."

Max laughed and headed to the sofa and plopped down, setting the bag on the coffee table. "I hope you weren't busy when I called."

Anna shut and locked the door and grabbed a bottle of water for Max before joining her on the other end of the sofa. "There's no such thing as too busy when Gino's lasagna is involved."

Max pulled out two containers and handed one to Anna. "What have you been up to? I haven't seen you since you brought me donuts. That feels like ages ago."

"Oh," Anna said, focusing on opening her container. "You know, this and that. How are things at the bookstore?" she asked to change the subject but instantly regretted the topic when she saw the panic flash in her niece's eyes.

"A little better," Max said with a sigh as she twirled spaghetti on a plastic fork. "The Christmas season has helped."

"And how's Robbie?" Anna asked.

Max took a bite of her noodles and didn't answer until she finished chewing. "He wants me to move in with him."

Anna's brow shot up. "So soon?"

Max lifted her shoulder into a lazy shrug.

"How do you feel about moving in with him?"

"It would save me money," Max said carefully. "My roommate's decided that, since she's out of the country so much now, she's not going to renew the lease. And everything around here is too expensive. That's why he suggested it."

Anna took a bite of her lasagna, then asked, "And if money weren't an issue, would you be considering it?"

Max shrugged again.

"I'm gonna take that as a no."

"Just because I move in with him doesn't mean it's serious," Max said, looking up at Anna with a pleading look. "It's only temporary."

Anna wasn't sure who Max was trying to convince— her aunt or herself. "Do you love him, Max?"

Indecision flickered in her eyes.. "I don't have to love him to move in with him."

"I'm going to take that as a no too."

"He's difficult, sometimes. Very passionate, but that passion can make him erratic. But I need to save money, Aunt Anna. I can't move in with Mom and her love nest, not that I even see or talk to her to ask. And I'm not asking Gabe and Sasha." She pushed out a sigh. "And before you say I told you so, I really did have all my budgeting on point until now. The whole roommate situation really threw a wrench in the works." She gave Anna a smile. "I confess I have an ulterior motive for being here besides bringing you dinner."

"I'm good with that," Anna said, expecting her niece to ask for help. "What is it?"

Max's mouth twisted to the side. "I was wondering if you'd had a chance to look for photos for the Bluebird Bay/Maine coast picture book."

That wasn't what Anna had expected, and she noticed the convenient change of topic. "Not yet, but we can look at them together."

"I thought you were editing before I showed up," Max protested.

"I was, but I can easily switch gears. Besides, I'm excited about the picture book too." She opened her laptop and a Dropbox file, then started sorting through some of the images she'd taken that summer as they both continued to eat.

But Max's casual announcement about moving in with Robbie was weighing on Anna's mind. She couldn't just let it go. "Have you talked to your mom about moving in with Robbie?"

As soon as she asked, Anna knew she hadn't. Anna had just spent most of the last week with Cee-cee and she hadn't mentioned it. Anna was certain Cee-cee would have, considering her opinion of the guy.

Max didn't meet her gaze. "I haven't had a chance."

"Have you told her about your financial issues? What about your dad?"

She shook her head. "Dad would definitely be telling me *I told you so*. I can't deal with that right now."

"You might need to shelve your pride," Anna said gently. "Maybe you could move in with your father."

Max snorted. "No way am I moving in with Mandy the Moper. All she does is complain."

Anna laughed. "I suppose that's a good name for her."

"I'll be fine, Aunt Anna. I'm here about the photos, not for you to figure out my financial situation. This is my problem, not yours."

Anna sat back on the sofa and turned to face her niece. "I know it's hard to admit you need help, trust me. I understand this firsthand, but that's what family is for, Max. To share your burdens, even if it's just to lend an ear or a shoulder to cry on. Your parents may not be able to help, but I know for a fact that they want to know. They love you."

Max pointed to a photo of a sea turtle on the screen. "I like this one. We might even consider it for the cover."

Obviously Anna's little speech hadn't been enough to convince her, but it had convinced Anna that she needed to take her own advice. "Max. There's something I need to tell you."

"Okay…" She sounded wary.

Anna picked up Max's hand. "Max, I don't want you to freak out when you hear what I have to say. Most importantly, I want you to keep in mind that everything's going to be okay."

"You're scaring me, Aunt Anna."

"I know. Maybe there isn't an easy way to ease into this. Maybe I just need to say it." Anna looked into her niece's worried eyes. "Max, I have breast cancer." When Max gasped, Anna squeezed her hand. "They think it's all contained, but we'll find out more tomorrow when I have surgery to have it removed."

Tears swam in Max's eyes. "*Aunt Anna.*"

"I'm going to be okay. I'll have to have radiation, but as long as it hasn't metastasized, I won't need chemo and that will be the end of that." Anna was oversimplifying things, and optimistic with others, but it was what Max needed to hear. And what Anna needed to believe.

Max started to cry, and Anna leaned forward and pulled her into a hug. "There, there, Max. Your Aunt Anna's too ornery to kick the bucket just yet."

"Why didn't you tell me?" she asked through her tears.

"I haven't told anyone except for your mom and your Aunt Steph. And now you."

"I want to come to the hospital tomorrow," Max said with a determined look in her eye.

"You really don't have to do it, Max. It's an outpatient procedure. I'll be home by tomorrow night."

"I don't care," she said, wiping her tears and steeling her back. "I'm your cheerleader, Aunt Anna. If anyone can kick cancer's ass, it's you."

Anna laughed. "You know, Max. That's exactly what I needed to hear right now."

Max winked. "I've got you covered." Then she turned to the laptop. "Now, about these photos. They're not going to sort themselves."

Anna watched her niece as she scrolled through photos, jotting down which ones she liked best, and Anna wondered why she'd held off telling Max about her diagnosis. She needed to take her own advice and share her burdens with her family, and she'd be ready to help them with theirs... right after she kicked cancer's ass.

Chapter Sixteen

Cee-cee could hardly sleep the night before Anna's surgery, and she was a bundle of nerves when she met Anna and Stephanie at the hospital. After the way Anna had handled the agonizing process of waiting for her cancer diagnosis, Cee-cee had expected to find Anna in a similar state. But the woman on the hospital bed was smiling from ear to ear and cracking a joke with the male nurse who was adjusting her IV line.

"Anna?" Cee-cee asked in disbelief as she walked into her surgery holding area.

"Hey, sis," Anna said. "Can you believe this guy's never been deep sea fishing? Lived here his whole life and never once tried it. I gave him Gabe's number and told him to hit him up."

Cee-cee smiled in confusion. "I'm sure Gabe would be happy to take him out." Gabe took clients out on his boat for deep sea fishing expeditions, and thankfully, he'd been fairly busy. Even in the off-season, clients still liked to go out on the water and cruise the coast.

The nurse finished with the tube and said, "You're all set for your surgery, Anna. We'll take you back in about fifteen minutes."

Anna's brows shot up. "Don't you want to draw on my other boob? Give me a matched set?"

The nurse laughed, taking her statement in stride. "I'll leave that up to Dr. Epstein."

Anna shrugged. "Last chance to see an old lady's boob."

"Anna!" Cee-cee protested while Stephanie shook her head with a grin, refusing to meet the nurse's gaze.

The nurse laughed. "Then I guess I better go find an old woman, if I want to see one." He winked, then walked out, leaving the three sisters alone.

"I see your orneriness is back," Cee-cee said, standing at the end of the bed. Even though Anna tended to embarrass her when she was like this, Cee-cee was relieved. She'd prefer this Anna to the broken one she'd spent the last week with. She'd take her sister either way, but ornery Anna seemed like the right person to get through this. Truth be told, Cee-cee selfishly needed the strong version of Anna to help herself get through it too.

"I prefer the term feistiness," Anna said with a grin. "Ornery sounds mischievous."

"If the shoe fits," Stephanie said in a serious tone, then grinned too.

"Okay," Anna said, holding up her hands in surrender, though she beamed from ear to ear. "Enough ganging up on the woman who's about to have a cancerous lump removed from her body."

Stephanie asked Anna a question about her Alaska trip, which Cee-cee knew was a way to fill the anxious silence. As the two discussed it, Cee-cee's mind fell back into the other topic that had consumed her waking hours over the past few weeks—the competition. She and Mick had created a list of cupcake recipes, over half of which were holiday-themed flavors, as well as designs. Considering that it was a holiday competition, it was a given the contestants would be asked to come up with appropriately themed, showstopping arrangements, which meant they could come up with plans for individual pieces, then put them together once they were given the challenge.

But as she studied her sister in the hospital gown, tucked under blankets and hooked up to tubes and wires, Cee-cee began to wonder if she had gotten her priorities screwed up. Her sister still needed her, no matter how good she seemed right now.

"I'm pulling out of the competition," she blurted out, knowing it was the right thing to do as soon as she said it.

Anna stopped talking midsentence and turned to her with huge eyes. "What? Why?"

"Because you need me," Cee-cee said. "You all think this has sucked up a lot of time now, but it's about to become all-consuming. How can I focus on the competition if I just want to be with *you*?"

A soft smile spread across Anna's face. "I love you for offering, Cee-cee, but I'm gonna be fine."

"We need to wait until after the surgery to decide that," Cee-cee countered.

"No," Anna said, lifting her chin. "We don't. I know it's all going to be fine, and Max helped me figure it out last night."

"Max?" Cee-cee asked in surprise. "You called her?"

"No, she came over," Anna said. "She brought me dinner and we discussed a project we're working on."

"I thought you wanted to be alone," Steph said.

"I did," Anna said, "but then Max called and asked if she could come over and I couldn't pass up Gino's lasagna. Or our project."

It all sounded reasonable, but Cee-cee could tell Anna was holding something back.

Anna cast her a blank look, confirming it. "When was the last time you spoke to Max?"

Cee-cee tried not to take offense. There was no condemnation in her sister's voice this time, so why did she feel defensive? "We text every day. I guess I haven't talked to her since last week."

Anna studied her for a second, then said, "Max had the idea to create a coffee table book of photos from around Bluebird Bay. Last night, we were selecting the photos that she'll arrange to have formatted into a book."

"What a great idea," Stephanie said. "I love it."

"I do too," Anna said, "and it's giving me a chance to spend time with Max."

Cee-cee felt chastised again, but, unlike at Stacks, this time there was no hint of accusation in Anna's words or tone, so was she just feeling guilty that she'd been so busy with her own life that she hadn't spent time with her daughter since Thanksgiving? Things would die down after the holidays, and then she'd be able to give Max more attention. Besides, her daughter was busy with the bookstore and her new boyfriend. Cee-cee restrained a shudder at the thought of him. He was everything Max had always previously avoided in a man. Maybe she was going through a wild phase like Anna...only Anna had never outgrown hers.

"You can't quit the competition, Cee-cee. You *have* to do this," Anna said emphatically. A mischievous grin spread across her face. "If this all goes south, I need you to win that fifty K to help cover my medical bills."

Cee-cee gasped. "Don't even joke about that!"

"Look," Anna said, turning serious, "once this surgery is over, there's not much else to do other than recover for a few weeks before I start radiation, which will be after the competition is over. So go blow the socks off those people, then bring home a big fat check. They give you one of those gigantic checks, right?"

Cee-cee laughed. Mick had told her the same thing—everything except the part about the size of the check. "I have no idea. If I win, as long as it gets deposited into my account, it can fit on the head of a pin for all I care."

"Then you definitely need to win so we can see what it looks like."

Cee-cee was about to tell her that if she made it to the finals, she'd get to see the check regardless, but an orderly walked in. "Ms. Sullivan? We're ready to take you back now."

Fear raced through Cee-cee's blood, and she turned to her sister in panic.

Anna held her gaze. "It's going to be okay."

"This is a turnabout," Steph said, her voice tight with emotion. "We're supposed to be the ones comforting you."

"And you did," Anna said. "Now it's my turn. I'm certain everything will work out as it's meant to be, and it fills me with peace."

Cee-cee threw her arms around her sister, squeezing tight as memories of their mother's double mastectomy surgery filled her head. No, Anna was different. They had caught it early.

"Promise me you won't back out of the cupcake competition," Anna said into her sister's hair.

"I promise," Cee-cee grudgingly agreed.

"Good. I can't wait to eat all those practice cupcakes."

Steph took Cee-cee's place, hugging Anna for several seconds. "We'll be out in the waiting room."

"I hear the coffee out there sucks," Anna said as the orderly started unlocking the bed's wheels. "I'm not sure what either of you have done to deserve that, so maybe go grab some coffee somewhere else."

Both Steph and Cee-cee remained silent as they watched Anna being wheeled down the hall. Once Anna was out of sight, they made their way to the waiting room, and Steph said, "Do you want to go somewhere else to get coffee?"

"No freaking way," Cee-cee said. "I'm not leaving this place until we take her home in a few hours."

"Agreed."

They settled in the waiting room as best they could, given their anxiety, both skipping the coffee. Cee-cee's attention kept drifting to the game show on the TV in the corner. She couldn't have cared less about who was winning or how it even worked, but she needed something to occupy her mind or she'd go crazy with worry.

She could tell Stephanie was worried too. She was quieter than usual and she kept checking her phone and tapping out messages. Cee-cee had a feeling this had nothing to do with Anna and possibly had everything to do with the receipt Steph had found. She ached to tell her sister not to worry about it, that there was no way on earth Paul would have cheated on her, but Cee-cee knew it wouldn't help anything. She and Anna had both assured her multiple times, to the point Steph was clearly sick of hearing it. Bringing it up again didn't seem like a good idea. It would only add salt to the wound.

Anna had been back in surgery for a half hour when Max showed up in the waiting room, holding a bouquet of bright colored flowers.

"Hey, Mom, Aunt Steph. Any word on Aunt Anna?"

Steph looked up in surprise and stood to give her niece a hug. "Max. I didn't know you were coming. I didn't know you even knew."

Max laughed but it was tight. "I found out last night, and Aunt Anna told me not to come, so you know that means I had to make some sort of appearance."

"You become more and more like Anna every day," Steph said, her eyes twinkling. "Come sit."

"I can only stay a few minutes," Max said as she sat next to Steph, and across from Cee-cee. "I was hoping you could give her these flowers and tell her I was here."

"Of course," Steph said, sending a curious glance to Cee-cee.

No wonder, Cee-cee thought. While Steph had risen and hugged Max, Cee-cee was still seated and she hadn't acknowledged her daughter's presence. She wanted to hug her too, but wasn't even sure Max wanted a hug from her. There was no denying there was tension between the two of them, and she found herself wondering how it had gotten there.

"That's so thoughtful of you," Cee-cee said. "How did you manage to get away from the store?"

Max tensed at the mention of the bookshop. "I got Mr. Bonomo's son Joe to watch it again, when I picked up a beautiful bouquet of flowers. But that's why I can't stay long."

The owner of the flower shop next door to Max's bookstore had taken an instant liking to her, and the two often traded favors, with Mr. Bonomo allowing his son to help her when she needed it, and Max taking in his mail and keeping an eye on the shop when he was away.

"Any word yet?" Max asked, shooting a glance at the door.

"No, Steph said, "but she hasn't been back there long. Last week the surgeon said she'd be back there an hour tops. Most of the time is prepping and recovery."

"So if I stay for a bit, I might actually get some news."

Steph placed her hand over her niece's and squeezed. "Let's hope so."

An uncomfortable silence settled over them, and after nearly a minute, Max said, "Tell me some stories about Anna when she was a kid."

Max had always loved hearing Anna stories. When she was little, Cee-cee always wondered if it was because Anna had always been so different than the rule-abiding Max, but now she wondered if it was because she really was becoming like her free-spirited aunt. How else could Cee-cee explain her quitting her job to open a bookstore and her current choice in boyfriends? Both were so totally out of character for the girl she'd raised. This version of Max felt foreign…uncharted ground that Cee-cee was hesitant to tread.

Steph didn't disappoint, regaling them with tale after tale of Anna and the crazy situations she'd gotten herself into when they were growing up. Cee-cee soon joined the storytelling and all three were laughing at Anna's antics.

Max checked her phone and frowned. "Shoot. I've been here nearly forty-five minutes and I need to go. Joe needs to get back to the flower shop to put together a big order." She made a face. "Shouldn't we have heard something by now? Hasn't it been over an hour?"

Steph's brow furrowed. "Yeah."

Max twisted her hands in her lap. "Will you let me know when she's out? Tell me how it went?"

"Of course," Cee-cee said, getting to her feet.

Max stood and looked at her mother before stepping into Cee-cee's open arms. Max held her close for a couple of seconds, then stepped back abruptly. "I've got to go."

She bolted out the door before Cee-cee or Steph could say anything.

"What was that about?" Steph asked.

"I'm not sure," Cee-cee said, still watching the door. She turned her attention to her sister. "Should we be worried it's been longer than an hour?"

Steph hesitated then said, "I'm not sure."

Cee-cee was grateful for her honesty, but as time continued to pass, they both became more and more concerned, until neither of them pretended everything was okay. At the two-and-a-half-hour mark, Cee-cee resorted to grabbing a cup of the sludge the hospital dared to call coffee.

Finally, about three hours after Anna had been wheeled back to surgery, the surgeon walked through the waiting room doors, his surgical cap in his hands. "Stephanie? Celia?"

They both got to their feet, even though Cee-cee felt like she was about to pass out from fear.

"The surgery went well," he said. "We removed the mass and we're sure the margins are free from cancer. We removed some axillary lymph nodes, and a frozen section of the first node, which we call the sentinel node, was also cancer-free. Something could turn up in the other two nodes we removed, but we would be more likely to see it in the sentinel node." He smiled. "All of that to say, I'm nearly 100 percent certain we got it all, and after a round of radiation, she'll be able to put this in her past." Then he added, "Not including six month then yearly checkups for a while."

"Oh, thank God," Cee-cee said with a hand on her heart.

"Why was she back there so long?" Steph asked.

"We had a glitch in the OR. Did no one tell you we got a late start?"

"No," both sisters said.

The surgeon frowned. "I'm so sorry. I told them to notify you. I'm sorry you were unduly worried. She's fine. She sailed through surgery just fine. As soon as she wakes up in recovery, the nurses will check her over and soon she'll be good to go."

He headed back to the OR, and Cee-cee threw herself at Steph and held on for dear life. Anna had dodged a bullet, and Cee-cee would never take her for granted again.

Chapter Seventeen

Everything had gone swimmingly. In fact, Dr. Epstein was so thrilled with the outcome, he'd told Anna before she'd left the surgery center that it was an "ideal outcome." She was sore, no doubt about it, but certainly nothing she couldn't handle.

So why wasn't she happy? She'd been so optimistic all day. Now that night had fallen and the surgery was over, though, the little seeds of doubt had taken root again. Suddenly, she was glad she hadn't fought Steph too hard when she'd insisted Anna sleep at her house this first night, at the very least. The hustle and bustle of a fuller house was a good distraction from her thoughts.

"Want some tea or something?" Steph asked as she made her way around the kitchen, cleaning up the dinner dishes. Pop was in the shower, and would be going to bed shortly after. They'd broken the news of Anna's diagnosis to him the night before, but he'd forgotten about it already—and it had hit him so hard, they'd decided there was no point in reminding him over and over again. He'd assumed she was moving slower than normal due to her fall, and that was fine by her.

It was only when she and Steph were alone that her sister told her about Eva.

"So after tomorrow, that's it for the foreseeable future?" Anna asked, stunned by the news.

"Yep. I wouldn't have even bothered you with it at all right now, but you'll be here when she comes in the morning, and I wanted you to hear it from me first."

"What now?"

"Great question. Tomorrow, I've got to break it to him that he's going to have to go to the senior center during the daytime so I can at least go to work and come check on you and all. At night, I'll just figure out how to manage him on my own, I guess."

Anna only had to look at the fatigue on Steph's face to know that, despite her words, that wasn't a viable solution. Not for the long term.

"I can come a couple evenings and you can go out. It will at least give you something of a break. I'll sit and play cards with him or something…"

"Stop," Steph said, her tone short as she leveled a glare on Anna. "You aren't supposed to lift anything heavy, make any jarring movements, or even raise your arms over your head, sis. If I'm not here and he has a dizzy spell or falls, what are you going to do? I'll tell you what. You're going to catch him, because you're stubborn, and then you're going to set your own recovery back."

"Steph—"

"Enough!" Stephanie tossed the sponge she'd been holding into the sink and rinsed off her hands with a shuddery sigh. "Sorry. I'm not mad at you, but we—Cee-cee and I—need you to just let us take care of this. We'll figure it out between us, I'm sure. You want to help ease our mental burden? Get well. Take care of yourself. And try giving us a little less lip while you're doing it. How about that?"

Anna had the grace to feel a little bit ashamed as she nodded and flipped open her laptop. "Fine. Consider the topic dropped, then. For the next two weeks, I'll let you guys work it out amongst you. After that, though..."

"Yeah, yeah, yeah, then you go back to badgering me again like usual," Steph said with a glimmer of a smile.

"You're a quick study," Anna said approvingly. As much as she wanted to help, she knew Steph was right. She couldn't do much other than be supportive for now.

She ran her thumb over her mouse pad and opened her emails, gasping when more than half of them were ads for Christmas sales. "With everything going on, I just realized I have done literally no shopping yet and Christmas is in like three weeks!"

"What were you telling me about those finger-knitting blankets your friend taught you guys how to do in Alaska?"

"That's right! I had planned to order a bunch of yarn and make a few for gifts." She tapped out what she needed into the search bar and found several online stores with a great selection. Steph rounded the kitchen island, and together, they selected a wide array of amazing colors, each with one of her loved ones in mind.

On a whim, she added several skeins in a rich hunter green.

"And who is that one for?" Steph asked, one brow raised.

Judging by her teasing tone, she already knew, so Anna didn't bother to play coy.

"Beckett, actually. He texted me and wants to get together when I'm feeling well again. I didn't tell him anything about the surgery—he just thought I was off because I'd had a long day and overdid it at the adoption event. I didn't have the heart to tell him I was in the grips of a midlife crisis and subsequent nervous breakdown."

The two of them broke into a fit of laughter that had Anna's chest and ribs aching in tandem.

Steph's laugh died instantly on her lips as she frowned. "You need a pill for pain?"

"Nope," Anna said with a firm shake of her head. "I'm going to take one right before bed so I can sleep. Now that I've got Christmas on the brain, you got any gifts that need wrapping? You know I'm the master, and at least I won't have to feel totally useless."

"Now, that I won't pass up. Let me get everything I've gotten so far from upstairs, and I'll meet you in the living room."

Anna closed her email and tapped the folder labeled "Alaska." She scrolled through the polar bear collection, amazed all over again by how magnificent the creatures were. Then she let her mouse hover over the folder titled "Misc."

She double-clicked and the first image that popped open was one of the arctic fox. Its grin and gleaming, mischievous eyes made her smile, despite all the trouble it had caused.

"Little scamp," she murmured. She was still flipping through all the images she'd managed to get of it when her phone rang.

She reached for it and peered down at the screen.

Beckett.

She paused, wondering if she should pick up. She hadn't told him about the cancer and still wasn't sure if she should. She didn't want to be treated differently. She liked that he viewed her as fun, fearless and maybe a little wild. There were few things less sexy than cancer...

Then again, who wanted to start off a potential relationship, even if it only turned out to be a friendship, with deception? Besides, she'd given Steph permission to tell Eva so they wouldn't have to tiptoe around her if Anna needed to stay at the house longer, which meant everyone was going to know soon enough. She was a great person, bless her heart, but she couldn't keep a secret worth a darn.

"Hello?"

"Hey, Anna. How are you?"

His voice was rich and sweet, and she found herself smiling as she replied.

"I'm doing okay, how about you?"

"Really good. Look, I know I said I would call you next week, but tickets are on sale for the Christmas Jubilee and they're going fast. I wondered if I should pick up two of them so we could go together?"

The Jubilee took place the week before Christmas and was a Bluebird Bay tradition. One that Anna had missed out on for the past ten years or so because she was usually traveling up until the last moment before the actual holiday. The thought of going, with Beckett no less, made her feel warm inside.

"I'd like that, thank you."

"Are you sure you're all right? You sound a little tired. Ribs healing well?" he asked, concern evident in his tone.

"Actually, now that you ask, I'm not all right," Anna admitted softly. "I'm at Steph's house recovering. I had a minor surgery to remove a cancerous tumor today, so I'm having some pain and I'm not quite myself."

The long pause had her on edge, but then he broke the silence. "I'm so very sorry to hear that, Anna. I had no idea. Is it…are you…"

"I'm going to be okay," she said, nodding to herself in affirmation. "The surgeon said it went great and my prognosis is good. I have a family history of breast cancer, so there's always a risk it will come back, but for now things look really promising."

"That's so good to hear. Is there anything I can do for you? I know you have your family all around you, so you probably don't need me, but I'm happy to do anything I can to help."

She thought about that and realized he was right. There wasn't a thing she needed. The gorgeous array of mixed blooms Max had brought her sat in a vase in front of her, right beside the box of cupcakes Cee-cee had dropped off on her way home from the shop. Her belly was full from the chicken pot pie Steph had made especially for her, and her heart was even fuller.

The image of the fox stared back at her and she blinked back tears.

"I'm good, Beckett. Truly. Usually, I'd already be looking for where I'm going to run off to next, but right now, I'm exactly where I need to be and I have everything I need."

"Don't hesitate to call if that changes," he said gently. "And if I don't hear from you before then, I'll give you a call next week."

"Sounds good," she replied. "Thanks for calling."

"No problem. And Anna?"

"Yeah?"

"I'm really glad you're all right."

"Me too, Beckett."

She disconnected and set her phone down, realizing she had a moony smile on her face.

"You have a cru-ush," Steph sang as she stepped into the room with an armload of wrapping paper and a bag of premade bows.

"What are you, eleven years old? I'm a grown woman. We don't get crushes. We get tricky bladders, gray hair, and a slower metabolism."

"Right. I'm going to let you off the hook because you just had surgery and whatnot, but we'll revisit this conversation in a few days. For now, come out here and work your magic on all these dang boxes."

Steph went and got Pop out of the shower and into bed. Then, for the next hour, she and Anna wrapped presents and listened to Christmas music. When her underarm began to throb and the stitches beneath her breast began to pull, she called it quits.

"I think that's about it for me, sis."

The pair of them stared at the pile of gorgeous, gayly wrapped gifts with a shared nod of satisfaction.

"Not bad. Teamwork for the win!" Steph said with a grin.

"I'd hardly call you handing me pieces of tape and shoveling bites of cupcake in my mouth teamwork, but whatever helps you sleep at night," Anna said, chuckling despite the pain.

"Hey, I'm not too proud to take advantage of free labor," Steph shot back.

After the week they'd had and the constant fear and worry hanging over them, it was nice to be able to laugh and for things to finally feel somewhat normal for a little while.

But when the gifts were put away and the music was off and she lay in bed alone later that night, the worries came rushing back in.

What if they missed some?

That's what the radiation is for, she reminded herself firmly.

And what if it came back?

She was usually a "knowledge is power" type of person, but she hadn't been able to bring herself to do the research on that yet. Her doctor had been focused on dealing with the problem at hand, so she hadn't pressed him on it either. If she were honest with herself, she'd admit that part of her didn't want to know the answer. She'd beaten back the jackals this time, but was that the end? Or were they circling around her campsite, just waiting for her to let the fire go out before they came and devoured her whole?

When Anna finally fell asleep that night, she dreamt of monsters...

Chapter Eighteen

Who hid my daggum shoes? Stephanie, I think your maid stole my shoes!"

Stephanie swallowed a sigh and finished tugging a sweatshirt over her head. She was just about to go downstairs and find Pop's missing shoes when she heard Eva snap back at him.

"For the last time, I'm not the maid, and you already have your shoes on!"

She sounded more irritated than angry, which was good, considering he'd probably asked her the same question a dozen times or more, and that would try the patience of a saint. It didn't hurt that, for some reason, Pop handled a tongue-lashing from Eva in a way that he didn't from anyone else. Stephanie grew more convinced every day that he enjoyed their scrapping and might even be pushing her buttons just to get a rise out of her.

Man, Steph would miss her when she was gone.

She finished changing her clothes and headed down the stairs. When she'd gone into the office earlier that morning to see a couple of the patients she hadn't been able to reschedule, Anna had been awake already and in the kitchen drinking her second cup of coffee. She'd seemed more reserved than the night before. Tired and sore, which was to be expected, but also quiet and contemplative. As Stephanie made her way into the living room now, she found her youngest sister pushing the pasta salad Stephanie had made her for lunch around on her still-full plate, seemingly unaware of her presence.

"Not hungry?" she asked softly so as not to startle her.

"Not really," Anna admitted as she set her fork down. "I was going to ask you, do you think you can drop me off at my place on your way to bring Pop to the cupcake shop?"

"Do you need to pick up a few things?" Stephanie asked as she took the seat across from her.

"Actually, I don't think I'm going to stay another night. I miss my own bed, and my darkroom."

And my privacy, Stephanie tacked on internally, sure that's what her sister was getting at. She could hardly blame her. This place was like a madhouse.

As if on cue, Pop started bellowing at Eva for combing his hair too hard.

"Jeebus, you devil woman. What are you using, a pitchfork? I can comb my own hair anyways!"

Even a war-weary-looking Anna grinned at that.

"Old charmer," she murmured with a chuckle. She lifted her gaze to Stephanie's, turning serious again. "I think I just need some time to process everything. It all happened so fast, and now that I'm on the other side of it, or nearly, my head is still spinning. I swear, if I need you or it's too hard, I'll call. Okay?"

What could she say? Everyone handled their pain differently, and if alone time was what Anna needed, Stephanie would make sure she got it.

"Absolutely. Let me get your stuff together. The paddy wagon leaves at noon."

Which meant she had exactly six hours of her own alone time left for the foreseeable future as Eva left for New York tonight. She'd drop Pop off so he could help out pass out samples at Cee-cee's for an hour or two, and Eva would pick him up, spend the afternoon with him and get him fed. After that?

She was on her own.

With a mental prayer for patience, she stood and went to work getting Anna's things together. She went into the guest room, surprised to see her sister had made the bed neatly, and even draped the peach throw over the corner. Anna had always said making the bed was a colossal waste of time. *"You're just going to get in and mess it up again in twelve hours anyway. Talk about a thankless job!"*

The mature, thoughtful gesture that Stephanie should've appreciated actually only made her worry more. She couldn't help but wonder if the past month had changed her sister in some deeper, intrinsic way. Sucking the vitality and spirit out of her so completely that she might never get it back.

Stephanie forced the thought away and tried to focus on the positive. Anna was in recovery mode. Who knew what good things the next few months might bring? She could just be imagining thing, worrying needlessly and borrowing trouble.

She glanced around the room to make sure she didn't forget anything and the bookshelf in the corner snagged her gaze.

This was where Paul kept the ones he'd already read but planned to reread somewhere down the line. Of course, down the line had never come for him...

As if on autopilot, Stephanie moved closer, scanning the titles, running her fingertip over the spines. If she opened them, what might she find? A note from a lover? Another strange receipt? Maybe a scrawled note in the margins?

She was teetering on the edge again, and any and all of the above would send her over. What had she just been telling herself about borrowing trouble?

Her sisters were right. The only things that mattered were that Paul had loved her deeply and that she'd loved him. She'd also trusted him. So what if he stopped somewhere for breakfast and hadn't mentioned it? That certainly wasn't a crime. She needed to stop looking for problems when there were plenty enough real ones to go around.

"Like how in the world I'm going to manage Pop for the next couple weeks without help from Anna, Cee-cee, or Eva."

By the time they were all in the car a short while later, her mind was working overtime trying to determine how she was going to handle this.

"Listen, Dad, I know we told you this before, but Eva needs to go away for a while—"

"Who?" he demanded, shooting her a thunderous frown.

"*Eva,*" Stephanie sputtered. "Your…"

"The maid, Pop," Anna piped in helpfully from the back seat.

"What's it got to do with me?"

Stephanie gripped the wheel tighter and wished Jesus could come take it right now. "I just didn't want you to be surprised, is all. There's going to have to be some changes. Starting tomorrow, you'll be going to the senior center during the day while I'm working. They have a great staff, there are nurses there who can help if you need it, and there are loads of activities each day."

"Senior center? So I can hang around with a bunch of whiny old farts complaining about their sciatica and bum knees. No thanks, I'll stay home," he said with a literal harrumph, crossing his arms over his barrel chest.

"That's not going to work, Pop," Anna said, leaning forward to pat his shoulder gently. "Your home is gone and you need someone with you—"

"Look here, little miss, I've been taking care of myself for over sixty-five years. Don't you tell me I need a babysitter. I'm not the one whose face looks like they went five rounds with Joe Frazier. I'll stay home and that'll be that."

Stephanie took a quick glance in her rearview mirror, veered to the right, and came to a skidding stop on the side of the road.

"Enough. I've had it! I can't spend every moment of my waking day arguing with you!" she said, pointing a trembling finger at their father. "We've all got a lot on our plates right now. Anna is sick, Cee-cee has a very important competition coming up, and we are smack in the midst of the chaos also known as the holiday season. You're going to go to the senior center until we figure out what else to do while Eva is gone, and you're gonna like it," she hissed. "Also, we're going out for dinner on Christmas Eve, and I don't want to hear a word about it. Understood?"

She caught Anna's wide-eyed gaze in the mirror, along with her impressed-looking thumbs-up, and almost let out a crack of laughter. It wasn't often Stephanie put her foot down, but when she did, she could be kind of scary.

"Fine," her father muttered, refusing to meet her gaze. "Maybe they have chess there still. And Mel from the hardware store said the coffee's real good." He paused and turned to stare out the window into the dreary clouds for a long moment. "I forgot about Anna Banana being sick..."

Stephanie's anger drained away in an instant, leaving behind a slick of nausea and guilt. She hadn't heard him use her baby sister's childhood nickname in years, and between that and the sudden wash of grief in his eyes, she felt nothing but shame that she'd yelled at him. It wasn't like he could help having dementia...

"Is she going to be okay?" he asked softly.

"I'm right here, Dad," Anna replied, rubbing his arm again. "And I'm going to be fine."

Stephanie swallowed past the lump forming in her throat and pulled the car back onto the road, making the rest of the short drive in silence.

"I'm going to walk him in and talk to Cee-cee for a sec. You want to wait in here and I'll leave the heat running, or come with?"

Anna shook her head and huddled back into the seat. "I'll stay. I don't want to run into anyone I know in there."

"Okay, be right back."

Stephanie led a subdued Pop into Cee-cee's Cupcakes, wishing she knew what to say to the old man to make him feel better and coming up blank.

"I know I'm a pain in the tookus, Steph. Everything just feels so muddled up in my brain sometimes, and I get mad...I'll try to be better."

Unable to speak for fear of her voice cracking, she nodded as they stepped into the shop.

"There's my guy," Cee-cee called with a wide grin from where she stood at the counter ringing up a customer. "Hey

Steph, hey Pop. Where's Anna?" she asked, her smile wavering.

She handed the customer his white box and a receipt, and he bustled out the door into the New England cold.

"She's in the car. She didn't want to run into anyone. She's all right, though. Not too much pain."

Stephanie was glad to see her father fall into his routine, taking off his coat and putting it behind the counter and then pulling out a tray to begin making up a small batch of samples.

Routine, she reminded herself. That was a good thing. Implementing that in her own home while Eva was gone would be imperative.

Speaking of which, she hadn't wanted to overwhelm Cee-cee with everything else going on, but she was going to have to tell her.

"You have a sec?" she asked, glancing around at the currently empty shop.

"Yup, perfect timing. We'll have a lull for another half hour, and then we'll get a little rush as people come in after they eat their lunches," Cee-cee said, wiping her hands on her lavender apron. She rounded the counter and made her way toward Stephanie, concern lighting her eyes. "Is Anna really okay?"

"Yes…well, physically. She's having a hard time coming to terms with everything. I think it's just hitting her. She's a trooper, she'll be okay. I actually just wanted to talk to you about Dad. Look, don't freak out, I've got it handled, but Eva's going to be gone for a while."

She filled Cee-cee in on all the details, and wasn't surprised to see that worry line reappear on her older sister's face.

"That's it. I'm dropping out. This is getting ridiculous. I know you guys want me to do the competition, but—"

"You're not dropping out," Stephanie said calmly. "You're going to go do this and you're going to win it. For all three of us. That's what Anna wants. That's what I want. And then, in a couple weeks, when Anna is well again and the contest is over, we'll reassess. I'm only telling you so that you don't hear it from Pop or someone else."

"Well, I've already got a new employee training. She's a grandmother and looking for something to do a few days a week, so it will be more than just after-school help. If I can get her trained in the next week or so, I should be able to take more time off."

"Which you will use to prepare for your contest, like you intended," Stephanie said with a firm nod. "But I'm really happy to hear it. If you can afford to keep her on, after the holidays, we can set up some days for you to help out with Pop."

"And until then? How are you going to handle all of this yourself?" Cee-cee asked, looking miserable. "Of all people, I know how tough it is, and it's only gotten tougher."

"You did it almost by yourself for the two years before. The contest is in less than two weeks. I can handle anything for two weeks."

Even as she said the words, though, she wondered if they were true.

Yoga was good. It relaxed the body, and the mind, and replenished the spirit. She was going to the studio the second she dropped Anna off. But it wasn't enough.

She replayed the conversation in the car in her mind once more and winced. If she was going to have to spend a lot more one-on-one time with her father, she was going to need to talk to someone. Someone who could help her do better. Be better.

It was time to find a therapist. Hopefully one who specialized in treating caregivers.

Armed with a new, decisive plan of action, she gave Cee-cee a quick hug and made her way out of the shop with a renewed sense of purpose.

She was in an unenviable situation right now, and she could either cry in her milk over it, or she could do whatever it took to make it better.

She chose option B.

Chapter Nineteen

Max was out of sorts. She'd already felt like she was walking on a precipice with her bookstore and feeling abandoned by her mother, but her aunt's cancer diagnosis had pushed her over the edge. She couldn't sleep. Her stomach hurt. She was always on edge. Robbie had been her current go-to source of distraction, but his appeal was starting to wane, not a good thing when she was preparing to move in with him.

Maybe they were in a rut. Robbie's idea of a good night was for her to cook dinner and have sex, although the order was subject to change. She needed to see more than the walls of her bookstore and the ceiling of his cluttered, undecorated studio.

Grabbing her phone, she sent him a quick text. *Hey, why don't we drive up to Pickford and grab dinner at that new restaurant?*

He didn't respond until nearly an hour later, but Max was used to his delayed responses. When he was in the middle of a welding project, he usually wasn't looking at his phone.

Pierre's? Isn't it pricey?

She pushed out a sigh. *Kind of? Maybe we could split it?*

It was an extravagance she likely couldn't afford, but she was hoping they could dress up and make it a real date. A romantic night out.

He didn't respond for another twenty minutes. *How about that gourmet hotdog place?*

Which meant jeans and T-shirts—uber casual, which was great, but tonight she needed more. She decided this needed a phone call.

"I'm busy, Maxy," he said in exasperation. "I'm in the middle of working on the McDermot project."

"Oh?" she said, trying to stay positive even though he'd been short with her. He'd gotten an extension and the deadline was drawing near. "You figured it out?"

"I might have if you weren't interrupting me every two minutes."

She thought about calling him out on his exaggeration, but it wasn't worth the argument. Robbie had a stereotypical artist's temperament—short and cranky one minute, uber sweet and loving the next. Only his short and temperamental times had become more and more frequent and seemed to be escalating. She told herself that his sweet moments were worth the cranky times and once he figured out this commissioned piece it would get better. Besides, he was loads of fun when he was "up." He made her laugh and she could forget the rest of her life was in the crapper. It was easy to get away with since she could count on one hand the number of times he'd asked about her day and seemed genuinely interested. But this was a fling, so it didn't matter, right? Only people didn't move in with their fling...

"I'm having a bad day, Robbie," she said, deciding to be honest. "I really need to get out and try to forget about things."

"Baby, I know how to take care of that," he purred, his tone soft and sexy now.

"More than sex, Robbie. I need romance."

He paused, then said, "You mean flowers and jewelry?"

"Those are gifts, Robbie. I need a night out. Candlelight. Dressing up. A date."

"A date." He said the words in a monotone that she couldn't read.

"I want to dress up and have you pick me up at my apartment and take me to dinner. Wine and dine me."

"We had wine and dinner just last night."

"We had a nine-dollar bottle of wine with spaghetti and jar sauce."

"It was dinner."

This was hopeless. His idea of romance was based on what position they tried. "Never mind."

Then to her surprise, he said, "Okay. If my Maxy wants to get all dressed up and go out to dinner, then we'll get dressed up and go out to dinner."

"Really?" she asked, her face warming with relief.

"Yeah. How about I pick you up at seven thirty? I'll make a reservation for eight."

"Thanks, Robbie. You have no idea how much I need this."

"See you at seven-thirty."

The rest of the afternoon flew by. She had several chatty customers drop in, and one woman bought gifts for all her grandchildren. After she closed the shop at five, Max drove home, buzzing with anticipation. She didn't even let her roommate's moving boxes get her down. She was going to be positive. Everything was going to work out great. Her problems with Robbie all boiled down to communication.

She told him how she felt, and he addressed the issue. See? Fixable.

She took a shower and curled her hair. She gave herself smoky eyes and red lipstick and put on a little black dress and a pair of black stiletto heels. When she looked in the mirror, she smiled. It felt good to dress up. This was exactly what she needed.

But seven thirty came and went and there was no sign of Robbie. At seven forty-five she nearly texted him, but she decided she wasn't going to chase him. He either wanted to go out with her or he didn't. She had kicked off her shoes and poured her own glass of wine, then turned on a movie. The wine had just kicked in, siphoning off some of her anger, when she heard a knock at the front door. A check of her phone showed it was ten after eight. Forty minutes late.

She took her time getting up and walking to the door, ready to chew him out for being late, but instead she was surprised to see he was angry. His jaw was tense, his eyes hard as they scanned her body down to her feet then back up.

"Why aren't you ready?" he snapped.

He was late and he was angry with *her*? "If you were here when you were supposed to be, I would have been." She turned around and was heading back to the sofa when he grabbed her arm and pulled her back. She caught a whiff of something floral. Was that perfume?

"I was working late, Max. It couldn't be helped."

She jerked her arm from his grip and put her hands on her hips. "What were you doing?"

"I just told you. Working."

"No," she said, "I want specifics."

His eyes darkened. "You want a minute-by-minute recap?"

"Sure. If that's what you want, but a general recap will suffice."

"I was meeting with the McDermot's," he snapped. "Trying not to punch Ian McDermot in the face when he mouthed off to me."

Her anger softened. "I didn't know you were meeting with them."

His shoulders fell. "Yeah, well neither did I. They just showed up and fired me. Now let's go."

She felt bad. He'd just gotten dumped by his clients and she'd been here pouting. No wonder he hadn't called. "We missed our reservation."

"I called and got a new one."

Now she felt really bad. He'd not only got fired, but he'd rebooked their reservation. "Let me just get my shoes and my coat." She slipped into her shoes, then grabbed her coat from the armchair she'd dumped it on. She half-expected Robbie to help her put it on, but he was too busy checking his phone.

"Maybe we should reschedule," she said. "When you haven't had such a bad day."

His body tensed again. "I busted my ass to get here, Maxine, and then called the restaurant *you* insisted we go to, and *now you want to reschedule?*"

When he put it that way, it sounded bad, but she wanted a relaxing night where they could talk and maybe he'd listen to her problems and about her day for once. She knew the night would be all about him now. Just like every other night. Still, if she cancelled, he'd be pissed. And if they went, he'd be resentful of having to go. She wasn't sure whether to choose option A or B.

"I'm sorry," he said when he saw her waver. "I know you were looking forward to this." He reached for her hand and enveloped it with his. "Come on. We'll have fun."

His mood swings gave her whiplash at times, but when he was sweet...

"Okay."

He pulled her into his arms and gave her a deep, soulful kiss, a far cry from the usual sex-crazed fervor that deflected their intimacy.

Was Robbie looking for more? Maybe moving in with him meant more than she thought it did.

When he pulled away, he wrapped an arm around her back and led her to his car, kissing her before he helped her into the passenger side car. Once he was out of the parking lot and headed to Pickford, he snagged her hand with his.

"Thanks for this," she said softly.

"You bet," he said. "I decided I wasn't going to let that idiot McDermot ruin my night."

My night. Just a figure of speech. The important thing was that he was taking her out. He'd put in the effort.

He launched into a long-winded version of his encounter with the McDermot's, getting himself all worked up again. The longer he went on, the more irritated *she* became.

"I had more customers today," she said when he paused to take a breath.

He shot her an irritated look and continued with his tirade until he pulled into the parking lot. Finally shutting up, he got out of the car and waited for her on the sidewalk with his hands on his hips and his face drawn with impatient look.

"Are you kidding me?" she muttered under her breath as she got out of the car.

When she met him on the sidewalk, he carried on without missing a beat. "And another thing, I could have been working on that new piece for my gallery instead of busting my chops for that asshat."

He wasn't going to let this go.

Noticing her blank expression, he prodded, "You know the new piece. I told you about it."

He'd told her about it ad nauseam.

"Do you think we could talk about something else?" she asked.

"I'm *sorry*," he said in disgust. "Am I *boring* you with the disaster of my life?"

"No," she said, "but I was hoping we could have a romantic dinner. I told you we should call it off and I was right."

"I'm sorry if my crisis is inconvenient for you," he sneered. "I just lost a ton of money, Max. Do you have any idea how much time and effort I put into this project? The only thing I earned for all my trouble was the deposit!"

"Which was two thousand dollars," Max said. "More than I've made in the entire month. Which you would know if you bothered to ask about my business." She threw her hands up in the air. "I can't believe how self-centered you are!"

He leaned closer and grabbed her upper arm, his eyes dark with anger.

"*Self-centered?*" His fingers dug painfully into her arm. "I had one of the worst days of my life, and yet I still took you out to dinner, just like you wanted. If anyone's self-centered, it's you." He shook her back and forth to prove his point.

She caught another whiff of perfume. Had Robbie been with another woman? "You're hurting me, Robbie," she said in a low, firm tone. "Let go of me."

"Do you have any idea what this place costs?" His fingers dug deeper.

"It doesn't matter, because I don't plan on staying." She lifted her hand and jerked her arm backward trying to pull loose, but he lost his footing and her hand smacked into his lip.

The next thing she knew, his free hand connected with her cheek with a hard open-handed slap. She saw stars as her knees buckled.

"Hey!" she heard a man shout, and in the next moment, two men were pulling Robbie away from her and shoving him against the side of the building.

"Are you okay?" a woman was asking, and Max turned to her in shock. What had just happened?

"I've called the police," another woman said.

"No," Max protested. "No police." She was coming to her senses and she was beyond embarrassed, although she had no idea why. She was the one who had been attacked.

"Maxy," Robbie cried out. "I'm sorry, baby. I didn't mean it."

One of the men shoved him harder into the wall. "Don't you talk to her."

Tears sprang to Max's eyes. How had she gotten into this predicament?

She dug her phone out of her purse.

"Do you want to call someone to pick you up?" one of the women asked.

Max looked up, the woman's face blurry through her tears. Did she? Aunt Anna couldn't drive yet, and she wasn't close enough to Aunt Stephanie to ask her. Her father was definitely out. She wanted her mother, but she couldn't call her and ask her to come and find her like this.

"No," Max said, "I'm calling an Uber."

"Max!" Robbie shouted. "Please, let me make it up to you. I'm so sorry, baby. I didn't mean to hurt you."

The men tightened their hold again, but Max said in a tearful voice, "Let him go."

The men gave her an incredulous look.

"I'm not going home with him," she said as she pulled up the app. "I'm getting a ride, but I'm not pressing charges." She had technically hit him first, and the bead of blood on his lower lip proved it. If she sought to press charges, he'd likely flip that switch from good Robbie to bad Robbie again and try to get charges pressed against her too.

"Max," he pleaded, walking toward her after the men reluctantly dropped their holds. "Come on. I'll make it up to you. We'll have a nice dinner, then I'll give you a back rub."

She released a short laugh. "You think dinner and a back rub will make up for this?"

"No, of course not," he protested. Then his eyes turned hard. "But if you hadn't been so confrontational, this never would have happened in the first place."

"Are you serious?" she asked in disbelief. She shook her head and pain shot through her cheek into her skull. "Never mind. I can see that you are. In case this isn't clear, we're through."

"Max, if you'd just give me another chance. You know I had a bad day, and I admit that I didn't handle it well."

"Didn't handle it well," she snorted. "Snapping at someone isn't handling it well. Hitting your girlfriend because you don't like what she's saying is domestic abuse."

"Domestic abuse?" he scoffed. "Don't be so dramatic. It was an accident. A mistake."

"You call her cut and swollen cheek a mistake?" one of the women asked in a cold tone.

Robbie turned to her, his anger rising. "How about you stay out of it?"

"How about you get back in your car and go away," one of the men shouted, jumping between Robbie and the woman.

Max held her breath when she saw a sedan pull up to the curb. The license plate matched the number on the Uber app.

"Thank you. Thank you all so much!" she called over her shoulder to the kind people who had come to her aid. Then, she turned and practically sprinted for the car, nearly falling over as she balanced on her stilettos.

Robbie spun on his heels. "Where do you think you're going?"

She opened the back door and shot him a look of disgust. "Frankly, Robbie, it's no longer your concern, because we're *done*."

He lunged for the door, rage on his face. "Don't be such a frigid b—"

She didn't let him finish the sentence, slamming the door in his face.

And that was better than he deserved.

Chapter Twenty

Cee-cee was in her happy place—in her basement kitchen making cupcakes with the man she loved and who adored her—yet something didn't feel right. She couldn't put her finger on what. She still felt guilty about participating in the competition, but Anna had insisted she stay in it. She was worried about Stephanie having to deal with Pop on her own. But most of all, she was worried about Max. Cee-cee knew the bookstore wasn't doing as well as Max would like, but her mother's intuition told her something else was going on.

"These are amazing, Cee-cee," Mick said, his words muffled as he took a big bite.

"They were Anna's idea. I just had to come up with the right recipe."

"Then my compliments to both of you," he said with a slight bow. "This is…amazing."

She laughed. "You already said that."

"It bears repeating."

She wrote down some notes in the journal she was keeping of recipes and ideas to improve them. This one didn't have many changes—a bit more salt and a tiny bit less maple in the frosting. She'd spent the past two nights trying out new cupcake flavors, and she was nearly ready.

"How's Anna?" Mick asked as he licked his fingers.

"She's doing really well. She went to her own apartment. Steph's worried about her, of course."

"What have you decided to do with Pop now that Eva is gone?"

"Steph's taking him to the senior center during the day while she works and is going to take care of him herself in the evenings for now. She says it's no big deal, but I know that she's lying. We plan to talk more about it once things are less hectic."

Mick was about to say something when they heard pounding on the door upstairs.

They both exchanged a look. "It's after nine, and it's easy to see that we're closed," Cee-cee said, glancing up at the ceiling when another round of pounding began. "Maybe we should just ignore it."

Mick pushed off the barstool. "You stay here and I'll check it out. I'll be back to help you clean up."

Cee-cee's stomach knotted, which was ridiculous. Bluebird Bay was practically crime-free. What was she scared of?

"Be careful, Mick," she said anyway.

He gave her a soft peck on the lips. "Always."

Then he bounded up the stairs faster than usual, likely because the pounding started again.

She considered following him, but then decided to start on the dishes so she'd have a clean kitchen in the morning. It had been a long day and she was ready to crawl into her bed with the man she loved. She'd started loading the dishwasher with the mixing bowls when Mick called down, "Cee-cee, Max is here to see you. Can you come up?"

Two things struck her. One, why was Max banging on the front door at this time of night? Why hadn't she just called? Then Cee-cee realized she'd left her phone upstairs after dinner. And two, Mick's voice sounded tight and clipped.

Something was wrong.

Anna.

Cee-cee bolted up the stairs in record speed, only to meet Mick a few steps from the top. He placed his hands on her shoulders. "Before you freak out, just know that I'll be all over this."

"What are you talking about?"

"Go take care of your daughter and I'll be back tomorrow." He gave her a light kiss. "Love you." Then he headed back up the stairs.

Cee-cee followed him and found Max by the windows overlooking the bay, her face swathed in the shadows of the partially lit room. She was wearing a pair of four-inch black pumps and the hem of a black dress peeked out underneath her wool coat. Her hair was curled and styled instead of her usual long, straight tresses or ponytail. She'd been dressed up to go somewhere, but now she was here. She'd never showed up at Cee-cee's front door like this. Not even when she was still with Nate.

"Max?" Cee-cee asked, her stomach cramping with anxiety. Her mind was running away with itself again. *Had* something happened to Anna? Or Pop?

Max turned and Cee-cee gasped when she saw the cut on her cheek and the blossoming bruise underneath it.

Max was here for herself.

"What happened?" Cee-cee asked, trying to soften the panic in her voice.

"Mom." The word was strangled as Max began to sob.

Cee-cee glanced over at Mick, who was opening the front door. "Let me know if you girls need me. I'll call you tomorrow." Then he shut the door and locked it.

She turned her attention to her daughter, holding her up as she sobbed. "What happened, Max?"

Her mind was running wild with possibilities, and Robbie's name kept coming to the top.

Max didn't answer until she started to settle down. "My life is a mess, Mom."

Cee-cee lifted her daughter's head to look into her eyes, brushing the hair from her uninjured right cheek. Her life hadn't become a mess overnight. This had been brewing for a while, and Cee-cee had missed it. "Come upstairs. I'll make some tea and we can sit down and talk about it."

Max nodded. "Okay."

They tromped up to the apartment, Cee-cee's heart heavy. How had she missed this? Had she become so focused on her own life that she'd missed the clues of how unhappy her daughter was?

Cee-cee filled the kettle as Max sat on the sofa and bundled up with a thick knitted throw. As she waited for the water to boil, she filled a zippered bag with ice and brought it tucked inside a thin towel to Max. Her daughter gave her a weak smile as she took it, then hurriedly dropped her gaze.

She was embarrassed. Why?

Sitting on the edge of the coffee table, Cee-cee picked up her daughter's hand and squeezed.

Max looked up at her.

"I have no idea what happened," Cee-cee said, struggling to keep her voice firm and not break down herself. "But this is not your fault."

Her daughter looked away.

Had Robbie done this? He was at the top of the suspect list, but blurting that out wouldn't help. Max needed to tell Cee-cee herself.

The kettle began to whistle, so Cee-cee got up and poured the water into mugs, doctoring Max's with milk and sugar before carrying both mugs to the sofa. Cee-cee set the mugs on the table, then slipped under the blanket with Max.

"Why don't you start from the beginning?" she said in a soothing voice, leaning over to pick up her own mug.

Max was quiet for several moments, and Cee-cee wondered if she'd need more prodding. Her daughter kept her emotions and worries close to the vest. Cee-cee hadn't realized how unhappy Max had been at her accounting firm until she had quit her job and announced she was already in the process of opening a bookstore. That was Max, and Cee-cee knew she should have been looking for warning signs while her daughter made this huge transition. Of course she wouldn't have shared her worries. That wasn't Max's way.

"The bookstore is an utter failure."

Once the dam opened, Max let it all spill out. The bookstore was in much worse shape than Cee-cee had realized. Max admitted that she'd kept it quiet because Cee-cee's business was flourishing and it made Max feel like an even bigger failure.

"You should have told me, Max," Cee-cee said, her heart aching.

Max released a short laugh. "What? And make you feel bad for me? It's not your job to make my business better, Mom. I didn't want to ask you for help like some little kid. But at the same time—and this is going to sound bad—I was jealous. And I was hurt that you were wrapped up in your business and Mick and the competition. I felt like you didn't need me anymore."

166

"Oh, Max." Cee-cee placed her hand on her daughter's thigh. How had Cee-cee let this happen?

"I know, I told you it was bad," Max said in a self-deprecating tone. "All I could think was that I went to college to learn about accounting and business and you went to college for English. I was the more qualified of the two of us. *I* should have been the one to make my business a success." She threw up a hand in frustration. "I made a business plan, for heaven's sake. You just started baking and opened your business. It made me feel even more like a failure."

"Oh, Max..."

"You must think I'm horrible." She lifted her tear-streaked face. "I didn't want your business to do bad, Mom. I swear. I just wanted mine to do better."

"I know that, Max," Cee-cee said, never doubting her daughter for a moment. "Of course you didn't. If the roles were reversed, I would have felt the same way. It's natural to be happy for the person you love and wish you had success too. It doesn't mean you want them to do poorly. You just want to succeed too."

"Yes," Max said, wiping her right cheek while holding the ice compress to her left one. "That's exactly how I felt. And if I'm honest, I kind of just expected you to know I was doing bad or force me to admit it. I kept thinking if you spent more time with me that you'd see it."

"I'm so very sorry you felt like I'd replaced you," Cee-cee said. Her guilt was suffocating. "I should have been there for you. I should have spent more time with you."

"No," Max said slowly, as though the idea was hitting her as she said it, "I'm not a kid anymore and I can't expect you to read between the lines. I need to communicate like an adult and tell you how I feel instead of expecting you to coerce it out of me."

"I knew something was wrong," Cee-cee said. "I should have asked."

"So we'll both do better next time," Max said with a smile, then grimaced, the movement obviously hurting her cheek.

"We'll come back to your business woes in a bit," Cee-cee said. "Tell me about what happened tonight."

Max's face crumpled. "I'm such an idiot."

"No, you are definitely not," Cee-cee said in a firm tone. "I suspect you got tangled up one step at a time until you found yourself in this situation." She paused. "I take it that Robbie did this?"

She nodded, keeping her gaze on her lap.

Cee-cee felt terrible. She'd tried to ignore Robbie's existence, thinking he'd be gone soon and she wouldn't have to acknowledge he was part of Max's life. But by ignoring him, she'd left her daughter in what turned out to be an abusive relationship. Her daughter who was reluctant to share the difficulties in her life.

"How long has this been going on?"

Max's face snapped up. "This was the first and last time."

Cee-cee felt relieved, but Max wouldn't be the first abused woman to make such a statement and then go back to her abuser.

"I know what you're thinking, Mom," Max said in a firm tone. "You think I'm going to go back to him, but I promise you. It's over. I wasn't happy anyway, and was starting to question my decision to move in with him, so this settles it. It's over."

"Wait," Cee-cee said, trying not to panic. "You were going to move in with him?"

Max started spilling her guts, telling Cee-cee about her roommate moving and losing her lease. How she'd started using her personal savings to float the bookstore, and Robbie letting her move in. That she'd stayed with Robbie because she'd felt so alone.

"I didn't know what else to do, Mom."

"Why didn't you come to *me*?" But Cee-cee knew the answer even as she asked the question. To come to her mother would have meant admitting how horribly things had gone wrong. "Max, I love you. I only want the best for you. I *want* to be here and support you."

"But you have your own life now. A great one with your shop and Mick. You spent all those years taking care of me and Gabe. Dealing with Dad. I don't want to be in your way."

"You will never be in my way," Cee-cee insisted. "You were my daughter before I had Mick or the shop, and you will *always* be a priority. Sure, I've created a new life for myself outside of being a mother and a wife, but being a mother will always come first."

"But you deserve happiness, Mom," Max said. "Even if it feels weird that you're finding it outside of me and Gabe."

"So maybe it's a bigger transition for all of us, more than we've admitted to," Cee-cee said. "You know Gabe likes Mick, but he still has a hard time looking him in the eye."

"Why?" Max asked in surprise.

Cee-cee laughed. "I'm not certain, but I suspect it's because Gabe realizes Mick and I are having sex and Gabe can't bring himself to consider it."

Max laughed and cringed at the same time. "I understand where he's coming from, but Mick's a great guy."

"He is," Cee-cee said thoughtfully. "And I suspect he's tracking down Robbie even as we speak."

Max's eyes flew wide. "What?"

"Yep. He mentioned something about taking care of it, although I didn't know what had happened at the time."

Panic filled Max's eyes. "He asked me who did this to me and I told him. I never thought he'd..."

"Don't worry. Mick won't do anything stupid. That's not his style, but I suspect he'll put the fear of God into him." The way Cee-cee felt right now, Robbie should be glad he'd gotten Mick and not her.

Tears filled Max's eyes. "I'm sorry I screwed up your night."

"You didn't screw up my night, and Mick understands. In fact, he'll be understanding when you move in with me until you're back on your feet."

"*What?*" Max shook her head, then grimaced. "I can't do that, Mom. You only have one bedroom."

"We can share a bed, or you can sleep on the sofa. We'll work it out." Cee-cee gave her a mischievous grin. "Although you'll likely only have me around half the time. I'll just spend the night at Mick's place...unless you need me, then I'll be here."

"Mom, you don't have to rearrange your life for me."

Cee-cee lifted her hand to her daughter's cheek. "I'm your mom. It's part of the job description." She got to her feet and grabbed a notepad and pen. "Now let's start thinking up ways to bring in customers to your bookstore."

Her attempt to distract Max worked, and she narrowed her eyes thoughtfully. "Aunt Anna suggested having you make custom muffins along with me opening a coffee bar. That will be a draw and another income stream."

"That's a great idea," Cee-cee said. "We'll give them cutesy, custom names."

"Aunt Anna suggested the same thing."

"See?" Cee-cee said. "We Sullivan girls are pretty clever, and you're a Sullivan girl too. Don't you worry, we'll set you back on track." They spent the rest of the night brainstorming ideas for the bookstore. Cee-cee realized this was going to take up some of the time she'd allotted for the competition, but she didn't care.

Family always trumped everything else, and she wouldn't have it any other way.

Chapter Twenty-One

Gorgeous.

Big, puffy, white flakes of snow floated down from the heavens, gilding the little section of cobbled street and the surrounding trees in what looked like powdered sugar.

Anna's first real snow of the season here in Bluebird Bay. Granted, they'd had some ice and sleet, and she'd seen more than her fair share of the white stuff in Alaska. But something about snow here, at home, felt special. Maybe it was the juxtaposition of the salt-laden breeze coming off the ocean and staring out at the shoreline that made it extra beautiful. Or, maybe she just felt happy to be alive today.

Anna lifted her face to the sky, sucking in a breath that was so cold it almost hurt. If only she felt this good all the time…

It had been more than a week since her surgery, and she was healing well. Almost superhumanly fast, according to Dr. Epstein. But her mind, not so much. She'd been plagued by nightmares pretty much nonstop, and they weren't going away. Not to mention working through random and very sudden panic attacks. One second, she was fine. The next, her heart was pounding, her hands were shaking, and she found herself slick with sweat, wondering if she wasn't having a heart attack. It was only her firsthand knowledge of exactly how debilitating panic attacks could be—after one of her friends and colleagues, Laura, had suffered a couple of them in Anna's presence—that made her realize what was happening.

Knowing what it was kept her from calling an ambulance, but it definitely didn't solve the problem.

She slowed her pace in front of St. Matthew's Church and let out a shuddering breath. It had been her primary care physician, Dr. Waverly, who had told her about the Cancer Survivors Support Group when she'd called to check in on Anna three days before.

At first, Anna hadn't even taken the time to write down the address and time for the meetings. She wasn't a big joiner, and she was even less of a kumbaya type of person. But as the days crept on, each with her feeling physically better but mentally and emotionally worse, she realized that losing herself in her photographs and finger-knitting blankets was only going to keep her disturbing thoughts at bay for so long.

She had to do something.

Straightening her shoulders, she swiped her boots dry on the welcome mat, shoved the door open, and stepped in. The pews were all empty, but when she glanced to her right, she saw a sign with an arrow pointing to the right.

Cancer Survivors Support Group, AA and Cub Scouts Meeting Room, the note below the arrow read.

She made her way down the hall, shaking snow out of her hair as she went. It was going to be fine, she assured herself. This was going to be a room full of people who had been through what she'd been through, and probably a lot worse. If anyone would understand…

The sound of voices poured into the hallway and she followed them, hanging a left at the end of the corridor. Straight ahead, she could see the room marked with a sign that simply read, *Meetings*.

She headed down the hall on numb legs, the whole thing feeling surreal, like she was watching herself in a movie. It wasn't until she walked into the room that the hum of voices penetrated the sound of blood rushing in her ears again.

The voices went quiet and she stilled.

"Hello, and welcome. Are you here for the Cancer Support Group meeting?" a blond, thirty-something woman asked with a kind smile.

"Yes," Anna said with a nod.

"Well, you're in the right place. We're going to be starting in about…" She trailed off and glanced at her watch. "One minute actually, so good timing. Come, hang up your coat, grab yourself a coffee or some water, and take a seat."

Anna glanced around the room, surprised to find there were more than two dozen people present. Some faces she recognized in passing, most she didn't, but it made her glad she'd told her sisters they could fill the rest of the family in on her diagnosis.

She quickly hung her coat on the row of hooks, ambled over to the table laden with drinks and boxes of cookies. She wound up pouring herself a cup of coffee, more for something to do with her hands than because she was thirsty. The sound of footsteps clip-clopped down the hall as she took one of the handful of empty seats.

She had just taken a sip of the piping hot brew when a snow-covered figure wrapped in a massive, wooly coat rushed into the room.

"Sorry I'm late. It took me forever to scrape the ice off my—"

Anna nearly did a spit take as she locked eyes with her nemesis, Maryanne Brown.

"Um..." Maryanne looked like she was considering moonwalking backward out of the place and hoping no one noticed she'd ever walked in, but by that time, Anna had regained her composure.

"There's an empty seat here," she offered quietly, gesturing to the folding chair beside her.

There was a tense moment and Anna wondered if she was going to leave after all, but to her surprise, the other women slipped off her coat and hung it up before taking the seat beside Anna.

Luckily, the attractive woman that had greeted Anna introduced herself as Elizabeth and began to speak, marking the start of the meeting, which gave both of them a chance to digest this new reality.

So Maryanne or someone she loved had cancer.

Anna felt an instant rush of sympathy for the woman that she tempered by reminding herself that, if she was anything like Anna, she didn't want sympathy. She just wanted understanding. They'd never seen eye to eye, and Maryanne had gone out of her way to make Anna's life miserable whenever she had the chance, but this common experience changed things.

At least, for Anna.

"We have a newcomer among us. Would you like to introduce yourself?" Elizabeth asked with an encouraging smile.

"I'm Anna," she said, clearing her throat. "I, um, recently had surgery to remove a lump in my breast. Just trying to sort of find my way with it all."

The others all welcomed her, and Elizabeth gestured around the circle.

"We like to keep things really loose around here. The members who want to speak do so. Others who just want to listen are welcome to do that instead. We'll give you a chance to settle in, and then you can decide if you want to share more of your story with the group. How does that sound?"

"Great," Anna croaked. She couldn't imagine spilling it all to a bunch of strangers, but maybe hearing their stories would give her some insight into what she was doing wrong. At the very least, it would surely make her realize she needed to suck it up instead of feeling sorry for herself.

"Why don't you go first, Cassandra?" Elizabeth said, gesturing to a woman around Anna's age with red hair the color of a new penny and soft, green eyes.

"Sure. I'm not gonna lie…it's been a rough week." Her eyes filled with tears, and she chuckled self-consciously as she swiped them back. "I finally bit the bullet and shaved my head."

Several people around the circle nodded supportively, as if they knew exactly what that had entailed.

"I could've waited, but watching it come out in clumps every day was like twisting the knife. It was sort of empowering to do it myself, you know? I considered rocking a bald head, but I don't know if you guys realize, it's December in Maine."

This was met with a bunch of chuckles, and Maryanne and Anna both smiled.

"Well, the wig looks amazing on you," Elizabeth said.

"I actually agree with you. My husband says he thinks I look like a sexier Nicole Kidman." Her grin wavered and faded. "But, uh, I'm sort of not so okay. Maybe it's vain. I don't know." She shrugged one slim shoulder. "I was pretty emotionally wrecked afterwards. Like I spent the whole day in bed, and it wasn't even a chemo day."

Anna glanced around the room, wondering if some of the others would turn their nose up at that admission, especially those who looked much more ill, some with oxygen masks and a man with his nurse beside him.

None did. Cassandra received total support and zero judgment.

On it went, with story after story. Several had Anna's eyes welling up, especially one from a mother who had lost her young son to cancer and another from a man whose wife had died just three weeks before at the age of twenty-nine, leaving him to care for three kids under the age of five while he grieved.

It was a tough hour, there was no denying it. And when her turn came around, she almost passed. It was only Maryanne's encouraging touch to the elbow that had her sitting forward on her seat.

She could do this.

"I feel like a big, fat baby, to be honest. Listening to how much so many of you have suffered." She held up both hands. "I'm cancer-free."

Everyone clapped and she shook her head slowly.

"Thank you. I'm so happy about that. But at the same time, I can't figure out why I still feel so afraid. And then I beat myself up for being weak when I'm usually so strong. It's like a vicious cycle, you know?"

That elicited two dozen knowing nods that actually made her feel a little less awful.

"I finally googled my symptoms, and I think I might be suffering from a form of PTSD. My mom died of breast cancer…I guess I'm just waiting for the other shoe to drop."

Saying it out loud was like letting the infection out of a wound, and she blew out a sigh.

"That's all I really have to say right now. I'm not sure how to handle it or what my next steps are. I'm just trying to come to terms with the fact that this might not be as cut and dried as I'd hoped."

"It's a very common response, Anna. One that can happen anytime between diagnosis to months after treatment. It's normal and there are resources out there to help. No pressure, but if you decide you need something more than the group meetings, let me know, and I'll get you some information."

Elizabeth didn't wait for her to answer, and Anna appreciated not being put on the spot. She also felt ten pounds lighter just putting her feelings into words and having others in a similar position validate them.

Amazing what talking things out could do.

Maryanne spoke next, and Anna turned to listen.

"I had my exam three days ago, and I'm clear. That's year five for me," Maryanne said, breaking into a wide grin as everyone hooted and hollered for her.

Once she'd forced herself to do some research, Anna had read that, for some types of cancer, the five year mark was an indicator that it was unlikely to return. She could only imagine how big that news was for Maryanne. What surprised her was how thrilled she was for the other woman. She'd said so many crummy things to Anna over the years, and had actively tried to sink Cee-cee's cupcake shop. Somehow, though, all those things seemed petty and silly now, and she cheered with the others as a happy tear leaked from Maryanne's eye.

The meeting went on for another fifteen minutes before Elizabeth called it to a close and reminded everyone that next week would be their last until after the new year. She then invited everyone to take the leftover cookies home before standing.

"Congratulations," Anna said to Maryanne as she stood and crumpled her empty cup in her hand.

"Thank you," Maryanne said, her blue eyes searching Anna's face as she chewed on her lower lip before speaking again. "You don't even know why, do you?"

Anne frowned and shook her head, nonplussed. "Why what?"

"Why I hated you so much."

Anna drew back, surprised at the other woman's candor. "I guess not. It just sort of…was. Like the Capulets and the Montagues," she said with a shrug. "And I'm sure I didn't make it better with my firecracker prank and my wiseass comments."

Maryanne let out a self-deprecating laugh. "Wow. It's so true about bitterness being like drinking poison and expecting the other person to die. This whole time I've been so bitter and jealous, and not only did it not affect you at all, you didn't even know why I felt that way."

Maryanne blew out a sigh and then laid it all out. How her boyfriend-turned-husband had been so crazy about Anna in high school and talked about her all the time. Maryanne later found out that he never got over it and used to make comments about how hot she was every time she came around. Maryanne even caught him stalking Anna's Facebook page for bikini photos when she would post pictures from photoshoots in island climates.

"He was a real perv for you," Maryanne concluded with a sneer that looked much more like the Maryanne Anna knew. "Ever since then, I couldn't help but compare myself to you. You had this amazing, globe-trotting life and a great figure that never seemed to find those extra ten pounds like the rest of us did after forty. I finally wised up and got rid of the guy, but I never got rid of the anger."

"Maryanne, I'm so sorry...I truly had no idea." Now that she thought about it, she did remember some inappropriate comments coming her way from Maryanne's ex over the years, but she certainly hadn't known that he actually had the hots for her and especially never imagined he talked to his wife about her. How disrespectful and cruel.

"His loss, Maryanne, because he's the one who drove away his super-hot wife. But your gain, because he didn't deserve you anyway."

"Thanks. I appreciate that." Maryanne arched a brow, her painted lips curving into a grin. "Now let's see if I can stick the landing with number four, shall we?"

Anna found herself grinning back at Maryanne. "Reggie seems to have a good sense of humor, at least. That's a great start."

Maryanne nodded in agreement. "He's a peach. I'm going to do my best to be a little nicer to him to see if I can get him to stick around. I'm glad you came today, Anna."

"Me too," she replied, realizing she meant it. She wasn't cured of whatever demons had been plaguing her mind, but she definitely felt like she'd made some progress.

"Can you wish Cee-cee good luck for me? I hear she's doing the East Coast Holiday Cupcake Battle. We'll be pulling for our hometown girl."

Anna agreed to do so and stood in stunned silence as Maryanne went to get her coat.

Well, that was a real kick in the shorts, wasn't it? She'd come to St. Matthew's for support, and she'd gotten a helping of that along with a side of absolution.

All in all, the best day she'd had since the whole cancer thing had begun. She might not be a rousing success on the whole ass-kicking front yet, but at least she was holding her own now.

It was a start.

Chapter Twenty-Two

"Y ou are not a terrible daughter. You are not a terrible daughter."

Stephanie muttered that mantra the whole way through the slushy parking lot, right until she reached the front door of the Briar Cove Living Center.

On the outside, the place was lovely. A sprawling, single-story building that looked more like a manor that might sit on a plantation in Georgia than it did like an old folks' home in northern Maine. The butter yellow exterior was offset by large, white columns, and cheery wreaths dotted with red berries decorated each window.

It was a good first impression, she admitted. Good enough that her feet propelled her through the door and up to the front desk.

It had only taken a few days of one-on-one with Pop to make her realize that she was out of her depth. She hadn't been lying when she'd told her sister she could handle it for a couple weeks.

She could.

It was what happened after that she was concerned about. There was no question that Pop needed to be *some*where with *some*one for the remainder of his golden years. Living on his own just wasn't an option anymore, no matter what they'd all tried to tell themselves after the fire. He was a danger to himself. If they left him alone in that house once it was rebuilt, and something happened, none of them would be able to forgive themselves. Dragging this all out was only postponing the inevitable.

Cee-cee was juggling a brand new business and an important competition. With Anna still in recovery and Eva gone, Stephanie was barely hanging on by a thread, even with Pop at the senior center most weekdays. Maybe if she was retired and had some time to herself during the day, with only the evenings and weekends to contend with, it wouldn't be so overwhelming. But after a long day at work, and then even longer evenings dealing with her difficult father, her life had become a constant grind. Cee-cee's panicked call in the wee hours last night about Max's crisis with her boyfriend had only strengthened Stephanie's resolve. Something had to give.

And still, the guilt weighed heavy on her as she introduced herself to the receptionist.

"Pleased to meet you, Stephanie. Will is expecting you. I'll give him a call and let him know you're here."

Stephanie thanked her and took a seat across from the reception desk. A man seated in a wheelchair wearing a hat and heavy winter coat gave her a nod and a smile.

"Hiya," he murmured.

"Hello." She smiled in return, eyeing the suitcase clutched in his lap. "Heading out?" she asked.

"Just waiting for my son. He's coming to take me home."

"That's lovely."

The elderly man turned his attention back to the front door, and Stephanie picked up a *Reader's Digest* magazine to read while she waited. So far, the place really did look great. The receptionist was lovely, and even the gentleman waiting by the door seemed happy enough. Besides, no decisions had been made, so there really wasn't anything to feel guilty about, she reminded herself firmly. Being here wasn't like some commitment. She hadn't even broached the topic with Anna and Cee-cee yet. This was a recon mission only…a far cry from a done deal.

Feeling slightly better about it, she waited patiently for another few minutes until a tall, handsome black man strode through the door from behind the reception desk.

"Stephanie?" he asked, hand extended as he approached her with a welcoming smile. "Will Foster, pleasure to meet you. You're considering Briar Cove for your father, Red, correct?"

She stood and shook his hand, reflexively searching his eyes for some censure or judgment but finding none.

"Yes. Still very much in the information-gathering stage of the game," she hastened to add.

He swept a hand in front of them. "Well, let's do what we can to help you with the gathering. Right this way."

For the next hour, he took Stephanie on a guided tour. There were two wings, one for residents who needed constant care and medical attention, and another for residents who could still largely care for themselves but needed help with bathing and other small, day-to-day tasks. Will took her through several different lodging models, which could be found on either wing. They came fully furnished, which was great as Pop had lost all of his things in the fire. One of the models was a double occupancy room meant to be shared between two residents, which was the most affordable. Another was a single room model that consisted of a bed—hospital or standard box spring, depending on the needs of the occupant. The last model was more like a studio apartment with a private sitting area and space to entertain. Pop would never go for constant care wing, but the other options were both spacious and quite nice.

Once they'd gone through all the features in each room, he took her to the common areas. Stephanie was stunned by the sheer number of activities in progress. In that hour alone, she saw a bingo game running in one room, an instructor-led chair exercise class in another, and a group of women quilting. Will handed her the weekly schedule, and it was just as impressive. A person could only be bored at Briar Cove if they chose to. Of course, knowing Red Sullivan, he'd choose whatever he could complain about the loudest, but still, it was encouraging. She also loved the fact that everything was clean and brightly lit and well maintained.

What sold her even more was the staff, though. They were so kind and attentive to the residents. Every time they walked into an area where a nurse or orderly was interacting with one of the residents, she was heartened by how patient and caring they seemed. Cee-cee was a saint with Pop overall, but Stephanie and Anna had both lost their cool with him at times. She wasn't proud of it and knew it was something she needed to work on. That said, it was a relief to see the trained professionals here seemed to have an endless well of both empathy and patience to draw from.

When Will took her to try the daily lunch special in the cafeteria, she was sold. She'd assumed that it would be set up like a hospital cafeteria. Instead, it was more like a large bistro. The residents were seated by a staff member and given a small menu depending on the color of their wristband. Green for people who had no dietary restrictions, blue for those with high cholesterol, red for low salt, and so on. Once they were seated and made a selection, their food was brought out to them on pretty, colorful plates. Stephanie took Will's suggestion and ordered the chicken Kiev.

"I seriously can't believe how good it is," she marveled as she forked up the last bite, leaving her plate almost clean enough to use again.

"I'll send your compliments to the chef," he said with a chuckle. "We take a lot of pride in our food and spend a good part of our budget on quality ingredients and restaurant chefs."

"It really shows," she said with a satisfied nod.

Her only regret was that Cee-cee and Anna hadn't been here for the tour. Telling them about it was one thing. Experiencing it was another.

Two more weeks. She'd muscle through, let her sisters get through their current crises, and then she'd test the waters by suggesting they come with her for a visit. If there was a better option, she couldn't think of it. Even once the Cupcake Battle was over, and Max was less traumatized, it wasn't like Cee-cee could sell her shop and drop everything to care for Pop. Just like Stephanie couldn't close her practice, and Anna's job required her to travel. They all had to make a living. It was just too much. Someone needed to make the tough decisions here. Of the three of them, she was the one with an already-contentious relationship with their father. If there had to be a fall guy, it might as well be her.

"Would you like to try some bread pudding, or a strawberry shortcake?" Will asked, interrupting her thoughts.

"No, I'm stuffed, but thank you. This has been really wonderful. You've given me a lot to think about."

"Why don't I have the chef box up another chicken Kiev and one of each of our desserts for you to take home? Then Red can test out our meal spread for himself."

Stephanie nodded and thanked him again. That was actually perfect. Got her off the hook for dinner tonight, and also would let her know if Pop actually liked the food or not.

She waited at the table while Will went to get her to-go bag. When he returned, he led her back to the front desk and instructed the receptionist to give Stephanie the full brochure packet with all the information inside along with his business card.

He disappeared back through the door that presumably led to his office, and Stephanie milled about as she waited for the brochures.

"He's late again."

She turned with a start to see the same elderly gentleman she'd seen when she'd first arrived, still seated facing the exit, suitcase on his lap.

"Oh, I'm sorry to hear that," she murmured, his pinched, worried expression making her heart ache.

He didn't reply and just continued staring through the glass.

"Here you go, Ms. Ketterman." Stephanie turned to find the receptionist standing at her desk, large manila envelope extended. "If you have any questions, feel free to call anytime," the receptionist said.

"Thank you . . ." She trailed off and leaned closer. "Um, that gentleman has been waiting for his son since I got here. Well over an hour. Do you think someone should call and check if he's been in an accident? There was some black ice over by Route—"

"Aw, yeah," the woman cut in with a sad smile. "That's Saul. He's there every day at this time. Usually between noon and two p.m. The first few months we tried everything we could think of to dissuade him, but it doesn't stick and just upsets him when we try to get him to leave. I usually bring him hot cocoa and a newspaper to break up the time a little."

"And his son?" Stephanie croaked.

"Lives in Seattle. He only comes twice a year. In another half hour or so, he'll remember and head back into his room."

The guilt this visit had so deftly managed to quell came back tenfold, and Stephanie went lightheaded with it now. Pop had memory issues too. What if he got confused like Saul, and spent his days just waiting for her or Cee-cee or Anna to get him and bring him home?

She knew she should respond to the receptionist in some fashion, but her throat was too constricted to get any words out. She settled on some facsimile of a smile and rushed headlong for the door, forcing herself not to make eye contact with poor Saul as she did.

What kind of fresh hell was this? Was that what getting old meant? Sitting by the door waiting for someone to rescue you from the prison of your own mind...someone who would never come?

Time was the cruelest of mistresses.

By the time Stephanie got back to the car, she was an emotional basket case. So distraught, no amount of yoga or meditation was going to help. She began to drive on autopilot, lost in her thoughts. It was only when she realized where she was heading that she began to pay attention so she didn't miss her turn.

When the sign loomed in the distance, her pulse surged, beating double time.

Pietro's Restaurant.

Today was already pretty high up on the list of terrible days. Why not go the full monty and see what other awful things she could uncover?

Chapter Twenty-Three

Anna was starting to go stir-crazy. It had been over a week since her surgery and she needed something to do that didn't involve photo editing. She was used to being in the great outdoors, but because of her restrictions, she couldn't do any of her usual winter activities like snowmobiling, ice-skating, snowshoeing. So she did the next best thing—she decided to skip her usual online Christmas shopping the week before the holiday and do her shopping downtown. Walking from store to store would be her outdoor activity, and she could bring lunch to Max and get the scoop about what happened firsthand.

Anna still felt bad that she hadn't discouraged Max from seeing Robbie. If she'd had any idea he was abusive, she would have told Max to run. She needed to make sure her niece knew that.

She sent Max a quick text, telling her she'd bring lunch by in an hour or so, then headed downtown to start her shopping. She hit a few stores, then picked up some tomato soup and gouda grilled cheese sandwiches from Mo's before walking to the bookstore.

Max was excited to see her and seemed happier than the last time Anna had dropped by. While she sported a bruise and a small cut on her left cheek, she'd done a good job of covering it up with makeup. They sat on the sofa in the middle of the store and dug into their lunch.

"Max," Anna said, needing to clear the air before she burst. "I hope you know I had no idea you were involved in an abusive relationship when I encouraged you to date Robbie."

"Aunt Anna," Max said in exasperation, "it wasn't an abusive relationship. We dated, he got pissed and hit me *one time*, and I ended it. End of story."

"Okay," Anna said, lifting her hands in surrender. "I just don't want you to think I suggested putting up with that was okay."

"Of course I don't," Max said with a snort. "Please. You're the last person I would accuse of that."

"So we're good?" Anna asked.

"We're better than good. We're great. I finally told Mom about the muffins idea, and she's all over it. In fact, she's already got Mick working up plans to put in the coffee bar, and he and Gabe are offering to put it in for me in exchange for free lattes for a year."

"Sounds like a great trade," Anna said. "And I heard about Mick hunting Robbie down."

Max grimaced. "He didn't exactly hunt him down, but he did put the fear of God into him and watched as Robbie deleted my number from his phone."

Anna laughed. "That Mick is a keeper."

"That he is," Max said with a soft smile. She hesitated, then looked embarrassed. "I thought that there were lines in the sand. Like Mom was with Mick or she was with me and/or Gabe. But Mick and Mom are including me in things and I like it. Mom being with Mick isn't the end of our family. It's just a little bigger."

Anna's chest warmed. "You have no idea how relieved I am to hear that."

"Me too."

They continued discussing plans for the coffee bar then Anna's Christmas shopping list.

"Speaking of shopping," Anna said, "I better get back to it."

"You're getting a Christmas tree, aren't you?" Max asked.

"What?" Anna said, then waved the idea away. "No. It's just me."

"You *have* to have a tree, Aunt Anna. We've got so much to celebrate. If you get a tree, I'll come over and help you decorate."

"I wouldn't even know where to get one." She'd never been in town long enough to bother.

"You just get the tree and I'll bring over my decorations. I don't need them this year since I'm staying with Mom. You can get a real tree at the nursery just outside of town."

Anna had never had her own Christmas tree, but she had to admit she was feeling more nostalgic than usual, and she liked the idea of being festive, as well as spending time with Max. "Okay. I'll get one this afternoon."

"I'll come over tomorrow night."

Anna left, her spirits uplifted. She finished her shopping, then headed to the nursery and picked out a small, five-foot tree and purchased a stand, then realized her dilemma. She wasn't supposed to lift anything over ten pounds for another couple of weeks. She could likely get the staff to load it in her car, but getting it out at her apartment was another issue.

"Hey, Anna," a familiar voice said. One that made her face flush.

"Beckett," she said as she turned to face him. Ho boy, he looked good. His cheeks were red from the wind and his hair had been blown into a windswept look hairstylists spent fifteen minutes fussing with on models. His dark brown eyes were bright and happy. "What are you doing here?" Other than seeming like an answer to her prayers from just moments before.

"I was driving by and recognized your hair."

She self-consciously reached a hand to her wild curls.

A grin spread across his face. "I *like* your hair."

Her hand dropped. This guy definitely knew what to say to get to a girl's head. "You getting a Christmas tree?"

"Would you believe it's my first one?" she asked with a hand on her hip.

"You're kidding," he said in awe.

"Nope. My niece and I are going to decorate it together."

"Does that mean you're busy tonight, then?"

"No, Max had plans. We're decorating tomorrow."

"So you're free for dinner."

She laughed. "You're a smooth one, Beckett Wright."

He held his hands out at his sides. "And that's not an answer."

"Tell you what," she said. "The guys here are going to load the tree into my car, but I need help getting it into my apartment. You help me with that part, and you've got a date."

"I can do you one better," Beckett said. "Instead of getting pine needles all over your car, I'll just load it onto the back of my truck and haul it over."

She almost told him that wasn't necessary, but smiled instead. "That would be great."

She paid for the tree and stand, and then Beckett tossed it over his shoulder as though it were a sack of potatoes and secured it on the back of his tow truck. "Lead the way."

The last time they'd gone out, they'd left straight from the pet adoption event and she had rushed off before he could ask to walk her up, so he hadn't seen her apartment before. Thankfully, she'd been so stir-crazy her place was clean and picked up. When they got there, he didn't waste any time getting the tree unsecured and up the stairs, setting it in the stand in the corner she'd pointed to.

"Would you like to stay for coffee?" she asked.

"I would love to, but I need to take a rain check. I got a call on the way over. A broken-down car outside of town."

She gasped. "You didn't have to stay and help me. You could have just dropped it off."

"And risk you trying to put it up yourself?" He grinned. "And don't you try to deny that you would."

She laughed. "Guilty as charged."

"About dinner," he said. "Pick you up at seven?"

"Actually, I'm so relieved I've been cleared to drive again, I'd rather meet you, if you don't mind."

"How about my place? Seven?"

His place. There was something intimate about going to his personal space and it scared her, but she found herself saying, "See you then. Can't wait."

And to her surprise she meant it.

***

Beckett already had dinner ready when she showed up promptly at seven. She'd expected a bachelor pad, but his house was well decorated and cozy, and she instantly felt at home.

"Something smells good," she said as she took off her coat.

He took it and hung it on a coat rack. "Nothing fancy," he said. "Italian meatball soup and Italian bread from the bakery."

"I'm sensing a theme here," she teased.

"I know what I like," he said quietly, his gaze piercing hers, and she had the idea that he wasn't just talking about the meal.

She glanced away, suddenly nervous, which was totally unlike her, but something about Beckett made her uneasy even though she felt herself drawn to him like she'd never been attracted to anyone before.

That was why he unnerved her. Something about Beckett felt like home, which was crazy, right?

"You don't have a Christmas tree," she said as her gaze bounced around the room.

"Yeah, I decided not to put it up this year. Teddy's into everything and he'd likely knock it over."

"Is Teddy your cat?"

He chuckled. "Teddy is my grandson."

"Oops," she said. "My bad." Although, for some reason, the mention of it didn't send her into the same fit of panic as the last time. More progress.

He laughed, and as they set the table together, she asked him about his afternoon. By the time they sat down to eat, Anna was completely comfortable and was enjoying Beckett's company when his phone dinged with a text. He glanced at the screen and grimaced.

"Do you have to make a run?" she asked.

"Nope," he said, still studying the screen. "It's not my night to be on call. It's a text from my son."

"Is it important?"

The phone rang and Beckett answered right away. "Hey, Austin. If you're in a pinch, of course I'll be more than happy to help. Bring him on over." Beckett hung up looking over at Anna in apology. "I'm so sorry, but my daughter-in-law is a nurse who works the night shift and my son's an attorney. He has a case that was out with a jury and they've reached a verdict. Austin's neighbor was supposed to watch Teddy if he got called back into court, but now her kid is vomiting. My ex lives in Vermont so I'm his last resort." Then he hurriedly added, "Not because I don't watch him—actually, I watch him whenever I can, and even have a crib for him in my guest room. I just told Austin I wouldn't be available tonight."

"Oh," Anna said, trying to hide her disappointment. She'd been enjoying her evening with Beckett, but she understood. Family first. "Don't you worry. We can reschedu—" Her words were cut off by a knock at the door a fraction of a second before it opened.

A young man walked in carrying a baby on his hip and a diaper bag slung over his shoulder. He looked like the spitting image of Beckett. "Hey, Dad. Thanks so much."

"That was fast," Beckett said as he stood.

Austin grimaced. "I was counting on you to say yes, so I was already pulling down your street."

"You know I'm always here if you need me," Beckett said as he reached for the baby, and he practically leapt into Beckett's arms.

"I really tried to find someone else." Austin's gaze drifted to Anna, who was now standing behind Beckett. "I know how much you were looking forward to tonight." Austin reached out a hand to Anna, which she grasped. He gave her a firm shake, his eyes beaming. "You must be Anna. I've heard plenty about you. Nice to finally meet you."

Anna's brow shot up as she grinned. "Oh? Do tell."

Beckett started ushering his son to the door. "Okay, that's enough out of you. Don't you have a verdict to hear?"

Austin laughed and glanced over his shoulder. "I hope to see you again soon, Anna. Melinda wants to meet you too."

His words were nearly cut off as Beckett shut the door on his son.

"Who's Melinda?" Anna asked good-naturedly.

"Austin's wife." Beckett gave his grandson a huge smile, his voice raising an octave. "And this little guy's mommy."

The baby giggled. He clearly adored his grandfather.

"Maybe I should go," she said reluctantly. The best part of her nieces and nephews was that she was never responsible for them, and was never alone with them when they were babies. She didn't get kid duty until they were older. Much older.

"You don't have to go," Beckett said as he put the little guy down on his sofa and started to remove his snowsuit. "You can stay and help me take care of him. He'll go to bed soon."

"I don't know the first thing about taking care of babies. As you know, I never had my own, and my sisters didn't trust me with them until they were old enough to rat me out if need be. Something about me not being responsible enough," she said with a nervous laugh.

"Nonsense," Beckett said as he picked up the baby, who was actually older than Anna first thought. He didn't look so breakable. "Teddy, this is Anna. Anna, this is Teddy."

Beckett moved closer to Anna, and the smiling baby reached out his arms to her, wiggling to be free.

"See?" Beckett said triumphantly. "He likes you, and it usually takes him a while to warm up to new people."

Anna stared at Teddy as though he were a gremlin about to jump out of Beckett's arms and eat her face. But the baby seemed insistent, so Anna took him so she could say she'd done her part and then get the heck out of there. Then a crazy thing happened. As soon as she pulled him into her arms, he molded himself to her and gave her a big smile. "Hey. He likes me."

"I told you so," Beckett said. "Teddy has great instincts."

Anna started making animal sounds and Teddy started giggling hysterically. The next thing she knew, she was on the floor playing with Beckett and his grandson, all thoughts of leaving out of her head. She helped give him a bath and even gave him a bottle until he fell asleep in her arms. Beckett took him and laid him down in the crib, and then it was just the two of them, alone for the first time in an hour and a half, yet she didn't mind a bit.

She let out a big yawn, surprised at how tired she was, but it was a good tired. A happy tired. A tired from being needed and wanted and she was reluctant for it to end, yet she knew she needed to go home and at least attempt to get some sleep. "I should probably go."

"Sorry about the interruption to our date," he said apologetically.

"I'm not," she said. "I love Teddy to pieces." Then because she wasn't one to play games or beat around the bush, she said, "I don't usually like babies, but I love Teddy. I'd love to help out the next time you babysit him."

Beckett grinned, creating crinkles around his eyes, but it only made him more handsome in Anna's eyes. "So is this a you'll-only-see-me-if-I-have-the-baby type thing, or will you see me without him? Because I'm prepared to sue my son for custody if it means seeing you as often as possible."

Anna laughed. "No need to go to such drastic measures. I think we'll want some alone time too."

Beckett closed the distance between them and slowly took her in his arms and gave her a soft kiss. When he raised his head, he grinned. "Agreed."

It had been a wonderful evening and she suddenly felt the need to give him a perfect date too. He'd shared his heart with her—little Teddy—and she wanted to do the same. "I get to plan the next date," she said with a grin. "I have something in mind. Something I think you'll love."

"I can't wait," he said. "But it doesn't have to be elaborate. Just being with you is enough."

She shook her head. "Nope. None of that cheesy stuff. And you'll see. It will be perfect."

But she knew he was all she needed to have the perfect date too. And to her surprise, she wasn't running.

Chapter Twenty-Four

"You've got this, Mom," Max said, shaking her fists in front of her as though she were shaking pom-poms. "You've trained for this. Be the cupcakes."

Cee-cee laughed at her daughter, expelling some of her nervous energy. "You make it sound like I'm about to go to bat at the Super Bowl."

Mick smacked himself in the forehead. "You've mixed up your sports again."

"What did I get wrong?" she asked, not really caring, but it was a way to keep her mind off the competition, which was about to start in ten minutes. She'd never paid attention to sports and had no plans to at this point in her life.

"I think you meant the Stanley Cup," Max said with a huge grin, and Cee-cee knew she was purposely vexing Mick.

It warmed her heart to see Mick and her daughter bantering like this. Max had always been accepting of Mick before, but after he'd confronted Robbie, the two had become closer.

"Are you nervous?" Max asked.

"Yeah," Cee-cee asked. "Are you?" She was allowed to bring one kitchen assistant and one carpenter to make bases, poles, or anything needed to be built for the expected elaborate displays for her cupcakes. Mick's role was obvious, but she hadn't figured out who would be her assistant. She'd almost asked Barb, her new hire, because she only planned on having her helper handle the easier, less technical tasks. Slicing berries, prepping pans, and chopping nuts. Then, on a whim a couple days after she and Max had bonded over the whole Robbie debacle, she asked Max. She'd hesitated at first, because she knew that her daughter would have to close the bookstore to participate. But then Anna had come through and offered to mind the store, freeing Max to help and leaving Barb available to man the cupcake shop. Cee-cee had wondered if she'd *want* to help, but her daughter had jumped at the chance. She wasn't an expert baker, but she was great at following directions. Plus she knew her way around a kitchen, and Cee-cee had given her a cram session the night before on what might be expected of her. Cee-cee had entered the challenge mainly for the exposure, but now she *really* wanted to win the prize. She'd planned on giving the money to Gabe and Sasha for their wedding, but now she wanted to give Max half to help her bookstore. It only seemed fair.

Because there were so many contestants, the competitors had been assigned to one of two groups. Group One competed on Friday and Group Two competed on Saturday. There were two competitions for each group—a two-hour challenge in the morning and a four-hour competition in the afternoon. Four winners from the second competition on Friday and four more from Saturday made it to the final round. All eight bakers would compete in an eight-hour bake-off on Sunday.

Cee-cee had been assigned to Group One.

Now she stood in front of three, at the front of the studio, she stood before her own L-shaped counter, which held a freestanding electric mixer and an electric cooktop. After a quick wave over her shoulder to the teams behind her, she'd introduced herself to the teams at her sides. She also had two ovens and shared a refrigerator and a blast-chiller with the two other teams on either side of her station. She'd introduced herself to both teams. One consisted of two laid-back sisters who owned a bakery in Vermont called Quaint Confections, and the other was a husband and wife team from Portland who clearly took the competition very seriously. The two sisters were joking and talking to the other competitors, while the bakers from Portland eyed everyone with suspicion as though they were about to steal their recipes.

Cee-cee took note of the name of the shop printed in red on their black aprons.

Not Fudging Around.

How fitting.

Cee-cee tuned in again as the producer continued to point out the available equipment in the room. There was a huge walk-in refrigerator with just about any ingredients they could want, but they were also allowed to bring their own ingredients to make sure they had anything unusual or a signature ingredient they might need on hand.

"Two minutes," a producer called out. "Everyone to their stations."

Max adjusted her Cee-cee's Cupcakes apron and watched her mother for direction once the instructions were given. The time was short enough that she wouldn't need Mick and his construction skills for this round. It was all on Cee-cee and Max.

The producer counted down and then the host walked out, beaming from ear to ear as she welcomed the contestants and the viewers who would see this aired right before Christmas. She explained the rules about the competition and how to advance to the next round. They would be judged on finishing the required number of cupcakes on time, the quality of the bake, and the taste of the cupcakes and frosting, as well as on the overall design.

Then the host announced the challenge and the rules. "This challenge is Winter Wonderland. You must make two different types of original cupcake. Then you must create an arrangement that reflects a winter wonderland. You have two hours to complete your challenge, and you may not use your carpenter in this round. You must use the items you were supplied with. Ready? The clock starts counting down…now!"

Half of the other teams were running for the refrigerator, but Cee-cee glanced at the tools and display options they'd been given and then leaned over a piece of paper and started sketching. "Max, can you get a dozen eggs and a pound of butter? We need to start trying to bring them up to room temperature."

"Sure thing," Max said, sounding nervous.

By the time Max got back, Cee-cee had made a sketch of a snowman made out of various-sized cupcakes and several trees composed of stacked cupcakes.

"Oh!" Max exclaimed when she saw it. "That looks amazing."

"The snowmen are peppermint and meringue-topped white cupcakes with vanilla bean frosting, and the cupcakes for the trees will be black forest cupcakes with cream cheese frosting dyed green."

Max clasped her hands in excitement. "That's amazing."

Cee-cee blew out a breath. "Not yet it's not. Let's get started."

Max found cupcake pans of multiple sizes, and she and Cee-cee started to make the mini cakes themselves. Cee-cee measured the ingredients since she knew the recipes, and Max ran the mixer and lined the cupcake pans with liner papers, and performed assorted tasks like crushing candy canes. Once the cupcakes were in the oven, they began to work on the icing.

Since the cupcakes were varying sizes, they all had to come out at different times, which meant Max had to stalk the ovens, continuously checking the cupcakes with a toothpick. Once the toothpicks came out clean, Max yanked the pans from the oven, then removed the cupcakes from the pans and set them briefly on cooling racks before moving some to the shared chiller. Unfortunately, team Not Fudging Around had taken most of the space in the chiller for their own cupcakes.

The host and the camera crew had discovered the situation from the sisters on the Quaint Confections' team and had come over to investigate.

"Do you think it's fair to shut your fellow competitors out?" the host was asking while the cameras looked to be about two feet from the wife's face.

She looked up in annoyance. "It's a competition. We're not here to make friends."

The host let out a short laugh and turned to face the second camera that showed the husband and wife duo behind her. "You heard it here first."

The camera then moved to Cee-cee and Max, and Cee-cee froze with terror. While she knew this was part of the competition, the thought of having a camera so closely honed in on her produced major anxiety.

"How are you coping with Not Fudging Around's strategy?" the host asked Cee-cee, both cameras focused on her.

She looked up at the camera with wide eyes, her tongue like a log in her mouth.

Max wrapped an arm around her mother's back and leaned her head against her mother's. "We're not here to make enemies. We're here to have fun. And if that team feels so threatened by us that they need to create a disadvantage for us and the fine ladies from Quaint Confections"—she gestured to the sister team on the other side—"then we both must be doing something to make them nervous. We'll figure it out."

One of the sisters ran over and gave Max and Cee-cee a high five on camera. "You know it, Max. Let's show 'em they're right to be scared."

The camera crew moved over to the vivacious sisters, and Cee-cee pushed out a long breath and gave Max a grateful look. "Thank you. I literally got tongue-tied. I've heard the saying before but never experienced it. My tongue refused to move."

Max shrugged. "I had a filmmaking class in college that involved being on camera a lot. I got used to it." Then, when she saw Cee-cee was still upset with herself, she added, "When we get through today, we'll have all day tomorrow to practice. I'll keep a camera on the whole time so it won't be a big deal. But first we need to win not one but two competitions today to make it there, so order me around. Tell me what to do next."

The next hour was a bustle of activity as the two women iced their cupcakes with white-as-snow white vanilla bean frosting for the snowmen and rich, dark green cream cheese frosting for the trees. Cee-cee had Max start melting white dipping chocolate in a pan on the stove. Then together they transferred the liquid to multiple small bowls and added food coloring for the carrot noses, coal eyes and mouths, and stars for several tree toppers. She also rolled out fondant to make scarves, having Max add royal blue and red food coloring to small pieces to vary the color.

They were given a two-foot-by-two-foot plank to hold their cupcakes, and Cee-cee had plans for every square inch. The moment Max had finished tinting the fondant, Cee-cee set her to work making royal icing to decorate the board while she finished making all the accessories. Next, they slathered the board with the royal icing, then quickly assembled the snowmen using dowel rods to keep them stacked, affixing the eyes, noses, and scarves, before they popped the snowmen onto the board, using the still-wet royal icing base to glue them down.

"How much time?" Cee-cee asked her daughter as she started assembling the trees. She'd used a leaf icing tip to simulate the look of leaves draped over the sides of each cupcake, adding to the overall effect as the trees came together.

"Twenty-minutes," Max said in a worried voice as she set to work melting dark chocolate to create stick arms for the cupcake snowmen.

The chocolate was ready to pour by the time Cee-cee had the eight trees assembled behind the three snowmen. She grabbed a small plate and poured thin lines, then shoved the plate at Max. "Put it in the cooler."

Cee-cee piped small dots of white royal icing on the green trees. Then she dropped coconut flakes on the frosting globs until they looked like snow clinging to the branches.

Using the same technique, she created snowdrifts on the ground. Next, she sprinkled everything with decorator sugar crystals, making the whole scene sparkle like a fresh snowfall. It all looked great—minus the missing snowmen arms—but it needed more.

"Max," she called out, and her daughter huddled in close, ready for her instructions. "Get some red fondant and roll it into five small balls. I'm talking small—like a quarter inch—then five more even smaller."

"On it," Max said enthusiastically, and Cee-cee was thrilled with her choice of assistants. Max was eager to help, and believed in Cee-cee enough that she took blind directions, just accepting that Cee-cee knew what she was doing.

"Five minutes!" one of the competitors called out.

Max had all the large balls rolled, as well as two small ones. Cee-cee took one of each and lightly mashed the smaller one onto the larger one, then grabbed a bottle of black decorator's paint and a tiny brush. Praying for steady hands, she painted tiny black dots on either side of the smaller ball and inserted a sliver of the leftover orange chocolate between the dots.

"It's a bird!" Max exclaimed as though her mother was the cleverest person in the world.

"Get the arms," Cee-cee said, putting a dot of royal icing on a tree and attaching the bird. It wasn't perfect, but it was the something extra the scene needed.

She had Max assemble the rest of the birds, including eyes and beaks, as she carefully pried the arms from the parchment paper.

"One minute!"

Max attached the birds to various positions on the trees as Cee-cee attached the arms. She had just inserted the last arm when a bell clanged and the host exclaimed, "Time's up! Hands in the air."

Cee-cee turned to face a beaming Max.

"You did it, Mom!"

"We did it." While Cee-cee wanted to win, if she never went any further in the competition, she would forever cherish the past two hours with her daughter.

The contestants were given a fifteen-minute break while the scenes were moved to several rectangular tables. Mick rushed over and gave Max a hug and then Cee-cee a hug and a kiss.

"You girls knocked it out of the park!" he said, his eyes dancing with excitement. "You've got this."

Cee-cee took a look at the other scenes and flushed when she saw that their scene was easily in the top half, but it wasn't only decor that won the contest. It was also the quality of the cupcakes.

She gasped in horror.

"What?" Max asked.

"We forgot to taste the cupcakes." They had tasted the icing, making sure the flavor was rich but not too much so. And they had tasted the batter of the peppermint to make sure it wasn't overpowering, but not the finished cupcakes with icing.

"They're going to be great, Cee-cee," Mick said, rubbing her back. "You've practiced both flavors multiple times."

He was probably right, but if they made it to the next round, she wouldn't make that mistake again.

The producer asked the teams to stand behind their scenes, then introduced the three judges—all well known. All were hosts of their own baking shows, two on a cooking network and the third on YouTube. The judges went down the line commenting on the design of the scenes and then trying cupcakes. They offered constructive criticism, and while it wasn't ugly, one of the judges was harsher than the others. By the time he reached Cee-cee and Max, he had trashed several teams, both in decor and cupcake quality. Max stood behind her mother and lifted a hand to her shoulder and squeezed.

The judges eyed Team Cee-cee's Cupcakes' scene and smiled, and the mean judge didn't look like he'd bitten into a lemon.

Good start.

"Team Cee-cee's Cupcakes," the bubbly host said, "tell us about your interpretation of Winter Wonderland."

"We wanted to keep it simple and fresh," Cee-cee said. "But have the cupcakes reflect the objects they were portraying. We chose black forest for the trees and peppermint for the snowmen."

"Don't you think that's a bit simplistic?" the mean judge asked with a smirk.

"Sometimes simpler is better," Cee-cee responded, trying not to let him rattle her.

"Only if you get the flavors right," he countered, holding her gaze.

Cee-cee gave him a bright smile. "I guess you'll be the judge of that."

The judges behind him grinned and several people laughed.

"She has a point there," the host said. "So tell us about the design."

"Again," Cee-cee said, "we went for a simple design and focused on quality."

"Quality over quantity," the third judge said.

"Exactly."

The judges discussed the various aspects of the design, complimenting her on the coconut snow and on the details on the snowmen. The mean judge frowned at her birds.

"You call these quality?" he asked with his trademark smirk.

Cee-cee's shoulders tensed. "I admit that we didn't spend the time on the birds that we would've liked, but we did the best we could with the time we had.

The host took a step forward. "And on that note, I think it's time to taste the cupcakes."

They selected several cupcakes, one from the middle of a snowman and another from the bottom of a tree. Then the host sliced the cupcakes, after which she and each of the judges proceeded to take a bite of the peppermint ones.

The silence lasted so long sweat began to form on the back of Cee-cee's neck. What if she chose wrong? Should she have ratcheted the flavors up?

"Oh my God!" The second judge exclaimed. "These are magnificent. Just the right hint of peppermint, and I love that the peppermint sticks are ground so fine it's blended into the batter. No chunks."

"I agree," the third judge said. "I would definitely feature these in my restaurant."

The mean judge had remained silent. "They're very good. Let's see if you held your own with the black forest choice."

They all tried the other cupcakes and had the same reactions, but Cee-cee waited for the mean judge's reaction.

He studied the cupcake, then glanced up at Cee-cee. "It looks like focusing on quality paid off. Excellent job."

Max grabbed her mother's hand and squeezed, whispering, "Good job, Mom! You'll make it to the next round. I know it."

The judges finished examining the last two contestants' entries, then spent five minutes conferring before the host announced they'd picked their winners.

"We want to thank everyone for participating, but only four teams can move on." She took a breath and then announced the fourth and third place teams, both of whom Cee-cee would have placed in the top four based on the judges' comments.

"In second place," the host continued, "is a team that played it safe but produced such quality that the judges were impressed." She paused and turned her attention to Cee-cee. "Cee-cee's Cupcakes."

Max nearly tackled her mother with a hug.

The mean judge turned his attention on her. "While your quality was excellent, we'll need more from you in the next round." To her surprise, he added, "I'm looking forward to what you come up with."

Cee-cee nearly fell over, and barely paid attention when the host announced Not Fudging Around as the winners of the first round. Cee-cee wasn't surprised. She'd seen their elaborate mountain scene composed entirely of cupcakes.

"One thing I'd like to add," one of the judges said, "is that baking is about teamwork and camaraderie. Freezing out your competition isn't the way to win. It should be based purely on merit. If you need to inhibit your competitors to win, then perhaps you're not worthy of it after all." Her eyes narrowed. "We'll be watching you in the next round."

The husband and wife team wasn't thrilled with the reprimand, but that didn't stop them from gloating.

They broke for lunch, then came back prepared for round two, which was four hours long and allowed participation from their construction support team member. The theme was Santa Claus Is Coming to Town, and Cee-cee turned to Mick with excitement. They had prepped for a Santa theme and knew exactly what to do.

Four hours flew by as the three of them worked feverishly to get everything done in the allotted time. Max started making the Ho-Ho-Honey and Buttermilk sponge with a cinnamon praline buttercream and the devil's food cake topped with latte-infused whipped cream frosting and filled with dark chocolate ganache while Cee-cee and Mick started on the construction. He made a platform for a sleigh and attached shelves to the sides so Cee-cee and Max could stack cupcakes. The sleigh had balsa wood runners and even a step for Santa to climb aboard. It took him nearly three hours to complete—and Cee-cee was certain it was only because of his skill that he did, but she and Max filled the time icing the cupcakes in various colors for the sides of the sleigh and then piping brightly colored frosting onto cupcakes to make presents, complete with piped ribbons and bows on top.

Cee-cee and Max arranged the cupcakes on the sides of the sleigh, red with a white stripe down both sides and around the back. Next, Cee-cee had Max flatten out a sheet of brown fondant as she piled a mountain of royal icing on the platform to secure the bag of presents. Once she had the presents in place, they wrapped the fondant around the royal icing base to create the bag, then cut out long strips from the remaining brown fondant for reins.

They finished with thirty seconds to spare, and the judges were beyond thrilled with their results, declaring them the second-place winners again, Cee-cee's cupcakes would move on to the final round on Sunday to compete with Saturday's two finalists.

Team Not Fudging Around came in first again, but that didn't diminish Cee-cee's excitement. She'd learned so much in both challenges, and she was ready to show up on Sunday to win it. But even better? She and Max were a team, and she could see that Max felt loved and needed.

That was the best prize of all.

Chapter Twenty-Five

Anna stretched her back and let out a low sigh of relief. For the first time since her surgery, she was in less pain than she'd been in since before her fall. She hadn't been sleeping much, but she'd take the good with the bad.

After the Cancer Survivors Support Group meeting the other day, she'd continued to research illness-induced PTSD and confirmed what she'd suspected from her early online searches. PTSD was a very real potential consequence for many cancer survivors, and it could creep in at any stage of the process. For Anna, it seemed as if it had been triggered by the surgery itself and realizing it wasn't the cure-all she'd hoped it would be. Her radiation treatments would start the week after Christmas, so who knew? Maybe that would be the step that finally allowed her to relax a little again and release some of this fear.

Her phone buzzed and she glanced down at it, lips tipping into a smile as she read the text from Beckett.

Out front.

She let out a chuckle. He'd told her, what with his big thumbs and often forgetting to bring his readers with him, he was a man of few words when it came to texting, and he hadn't been kidding. Still, just the two managed to make the butterflies in her belly start flapping.

Steph was right. She had a crush. A big one. They'd had a great time the other day, even after his grandson had shown up, and she was really looking forward to their afternoon together. It was going to be a low-key date by her design. The two of them heading out into the woods behind his house and taking pictures of the snow on the trees. Beckett was just learning the basics of photography, and who better to help him learn than Anna? He'd hesitated when she'd told him about her date plan because he didn't want her overdoing it, but she'd insisted. The doctor had cleared her for leisurely walking, and she was desperate for some activity, so he'd finally relented.

She scooped up her camera bag and backpack, then headed down to meet him. He had pulled up and double-parked right in front of her building to keep her from having to walk out to the icy parking lot, and she marveled at how considerate he was.

"Aren't you pretty," he said in his gruff tone as she slid into the passenger's seat of his truck.

Her facial bruising was all but gone now, and she'd hidden the rest under a thin layer of powder. That, a sweep of mascara, and a swipe of lip gloss had been about the extent of her makeup routine, but the fact that he'd noticed and appreciated the effort made her grin.

"You're looking rather nice yourself."

Unlike Anna who was ensconced in a puffy, winter-white coat and matching gloves, Beckett, having been in the heated cab of his truck on the ride over, had stripped down to just his flannel shirt and well-worn jeans.

Then again, every pair of Beckett's jeans were worn well. As he pulled smoothly into traffic, Anna took the liberty of giving him a furtive once-over, admiring the broadness of his shoulders and the square line of his jaw.

He looked like he belonged in a commercial for something manly like motor oil or grilling charcoal, and she had to admit, she didn't hate it.

"I'm going to ask you one more time, because I'm stubborn like that. I'm really excited for you to teach me, but you sure you're feeling up to this?" he said, glancing over at her as he weaved his way through traffic toward the road leading away from downtown Bluebird Bay.

"One hundred percent. And if I start to feel sore, we'll go inside. I'm not trying to be a hero, Beckett. I just haven't taken any photos in a while, and I'm itching to get out there."

He nodded, clearly satisfied with her answer. On the ten-minute ride to his house, they chatted easily. Anna talked over the various selections she'd made for the coffee table book she and Max were working on, and Beckett had her smiling like a fool as he told her about an elderly woman who didn't have the cash to pay him for towing her old station wagon, so she'd opted to pay him in pies. The first, apple and sour cream, was waiting at Beckett's place, along with some hot cider, for them to have after they finished taking photographs.

By the time they pulled into his driveway, she was feeling better than she'd felt all morning. Just the promise of a little time away from all the recent drama in her life had her almost giddy.

The two of them piled out of the truck and made their way toward the house as Beckett tugged on his coat. They'd just reached the porch when Anna stopped in her tracks.

"Shhhh, wait," she whispered, crooking her index finger at him when he met her gaze.

To his credit, he complied, soundlessly closing the distance between them.

"What do you see?" he whispered back.

"Moose at three o'clock."

Beckett turned to his right and followed the direction of her now-pointing finger.

She knew the second he saw it, barely camouflaged by a massive jack pine in the distance. He let out a sigh of wonder and instantly reached for his camera slung over his shoulder.

Anna did the same, and side by side, they crept stealthily closer…but not too close. In Maine, moose were similar to hippos in Africa. Tourists often assumed that, because they looked sweet and cuddly, they could walk right up to them. In fact, they were one of the most dangerous animals in the state. Between the number of people who hit them with their cars and the handful of defensive attacks, more people were injured by moose each year than black bears in many parts of the state.

A lifelong Mainer, Beckett was clearly aware of that little bit of trivia, because he didn't seem keen for them to get much closer as they tugged out their cameras and pulled off the lens covers.

"The key with wildlife especially is to take a lot of shots. You never know which moment is going to be the special one that stands out, so I click like mad," she explained as she did just that. "This is the perfect time of day. We call it the golden hour. It refers to the two windows of time just after the sun rises and before the sun sets, when there's this soft, beautiful, golden wash over everything…like nature's filter, if you will. It's supposed to be about an hour long, but up here this far north, it lasts longer in the winter time. We should have a good ninety minutes or so of just amazing lighting."

Beckett proved to be an excellent pupil, asking all the right questions and soaking it all in like a sponge. For the rest of the late afternoon, she didn't think about cancer even once. If it hadn't gotten too dark and their fingers weren't like miniature blocks of ice, they might have even stayed out longer.

They tromped up the snowy path from Beckett's massive backyard, his hand on her elbow as he guided her. That might've annoyed the old Anna. She was fit, agile, and smart enough to wear good, sturdy boots. She'd also traveled the world in far harsher climates without a man's help. But post-fall Anna felt nothing but appreciation for his protective gesture. She'd had good, sturdy boots on in Alaska, too, right before she went toppling down that hill. Plus, somehow, when Beckett did it, it felt different. He never talked down, or little-lady'ed her. He treated her like his equal. Albeit, an equal with some bum ribs and a penchant for slipping.

"I know it's not possible, but I swear, I can smell that apple pie from here," Anna said with a chuckle as they stomped their shoes on the back porch before heading into the house.

"You're preaching to the choir. Why don't you take your boots off and get comfortable while I dish us up a couple slabs and heat the cider." His cheeks were ruddy from the cold, and the tip of his long, straight nose was red, and she found herself fighting the urge to lean up and kiss it.

Instead, she cleared her throat and nodded, turning to make her way into the little mudroom. "Don't threaten me with a good time!"

This was good. She liked Beckett more and more each time they got together, so what was holding her back from jumping in with both feet? That had never been a problem for her in the past.

"I'm adding some cinnamon and clove, sound good?" he called from the kitchen.

"Perfect!"

And it was. So she refused to muck it all up with deep thoughts and doubt. Instead, she was going to enjoy the good feelings while they lasted. Because when she was alone in her bed late at night, the monsters would be back, and this magic moment with her new crush would seem light-years away.

She yanked off her boots and coat and made her way into the kitchen. "How can I help?"

Ten minutes later, they were comfortably seated side by side on the couch, working their way through two colossal pieces of the hot apple pie...the best Anna had ever tasted. She made a mental note to tell Cee-cee about potentially testing a new cupcake with a sour cream and apple filling.

She forked up another bite and then reached for her cell phone. Today was the first day of competition, and she'd heard from Cee-cee earlier that morning—she and Max had done really well and had moved on to phase two—but she'd hoped to hear from her about how the afternoon portion of things had gone. So far, there had been no word.

"Everything okay?" Beckett asked.

"Yup, just checking to see if Cee-cee texted."

"I've had her cupcakes, and if there are better ones out there, I'd be pretty shocked. She's going to do great."

"I hope so. She really needs this. Not literally, but just for her own self-confidence. Plus, after everything that Max has been going through, I think this will be a really great bonding experience for them. Winning would be...well, icing on the cake," she said with a chuckle.

Beckett smiled at her and ate the last of his pie with a satisfied sigh.

"I can't deny it, it's been a pretty perfect date so far. Getting lessons from renowned wildlife photographer Anna Sullivan, having pie and cider for dinner, and getting to spend a quiet evening at home with my best girl? I'm a happy guy."

Anna cleared her suddenly dry throat and tried not to let herself get into a tizzy. So he'd called her his best girl. An old-fashioned figure of speech. They'd been on a few dates and she'd met his grandson, no big deal.

Only it felt like a very big deal.

Again, she found herself wanting to lean into it instead of away.

"Actually, I brought you a couple little things. Early Christmas gifts," she said, standing and making her way back into the kitchen where she'd left her backpack. She rifled through it and came out with two gaily wrapped packages topped off with elaborate bows. She brought them into the living room and handed them to a stunned Beckett.

"You weren't kidding. Anna, it's not even Christmas. But more to the point, I haven't gotten anything for you yet," he protested.

She shrugged and took her seat beside him again, anticipation fluttering in her belly. "It's really no big deal, just one thing relating to our afternoon, and the other I thought would be fitting for tonight."

Despite his initial protest, he opened the first with the relish of a little boy, and again she found herself utterly charmed by him.

"A book on photography," he murmured, clearly pleased as he began to leaf through it.

"Yup, it's a really comprehensive guide for beginners. And I'm actually featured in it. If you go to page eighty-seven, I contributed the chapter on lighting. It sort of reiterates and elaborates on everything we talked about today. I was thinking when we...uh, if we do it again, we could sort of work through some of the lessons together."

"This is probably one of the most thoughtful gifts I've ever gotten," he said, his voice husky as he closed the cover of the book.

"Open the next one now!" she said, as much because she was excited for him to see her handiwork as she was to slow this spinning-top feeling rolling over her. She was crushing and she was crushing hard.

Beckett set the book on the table and turned his attention to the larger package. He tore it open and pulled out the contents.

"Nice! It's so soft, and I love the color," he said as he rubbed the hunter green throw between his thumb and forefinger.

Her cheeks heated with pleasure. "Yeah, I thought it might be a good color for you when I saw the yarn, and now that I've been to your house, I'm thrilled to see I was right." She gestured around her to the dark wood and cabin-like feel of Beckett's masculine home.

"Wait. You made this?" he asked with a start.

"I did. With these two hands," she said, holding them up solemnly, like a surgeon.

He let out a long, low whistle. "You set the bar really high, so I'm going to have some major thinking to do now. You are a woman of many talents."

He looked like he wanted to say more but then went quiet, leaning slowly, inexorably closer.

"Seriously. Thank you," he murmured a second before his lips touched hers. It was a sweet, tender kiss that made her feel achy and content all at once. She let her arms slip around his neck and returned it with as much passion as she could muster. She was just really getting into it when she pressed herself flush against his muscular chest and sent a shaft of pain through her ribs that had her gasping.

She tried to keep him close anyway, but Beckett pulled away with a regretful sigh. "Anna…I know you were cleared to drive, but you definitely weren't cleared to crush those poor ribs against a big, clumsy guy on a couch. What say we find a Christmas movie to watch, I pop some corn, and we climb under that blanket and snuggle up together?"

She wanted to kick herself for gasping. Already the pain was gone, but it was too late, and Beckett was too much of a gentleman to be swayed.

She pressed her forehead against his and nodded. "Extra butter?"

"Extra butter," he promised before dropping a kiss on her temple and standing.

It wasn't until he left the room that she flopped back against the couch and giggled like a teenage girl. So what if she had a gray hair? So what if her back got sore and she had hot flashes once in a while? She'd had a great life, but maybe things didn't have to be the same as they'd always been for it to continue being great. Maybe it was time to grow a little. Change from a butterfly into another kind of slightly less active butterfly…with crow's feet.

Now, if she could just recapture this feeling later tonight, when she was alone in her bed and the nightmares returned? She'd be cooking with gas.

Chapter Twenty-Six

It looks like every strip club in a fifty-mile radius dumped their leftover tassels in the trash can and you picked 'em up and stuck 'em on that tree."

Stephanie closed her eyes and prayed for strength as she turned to face a scowling Pop.

"Thanks, Dad. When I was dragging this eight-foot monstrosity from the attic and spending my whole afternoon decorating it, I was trying to think of what vibe to go for, and you nailed it. Burlesque chic. It's all the rage."

He shrugged and waved a dismissive hand before bobbling back into his bedroom and slamming the door.

He'd been even more out of sorts than normal since Eva left, and that was saying something. Their bickering had gotten so bad that Stephanie had to leave the house to get some air a few hours before. She'd stood outside for twenty minutes to cool down—literally—before she was able to get into a good headspace to deal with him again.

She'd taken out and put away the brochures for Briar Cove more times than she could count, but she couldn't seem to come to a decision. Sometimes in life there were no perfect solutions and a body had to settle for the thing that sucked the least.

Tonight, she was relying on her sisters to help her figure out what that was.

She'd wanted to wait until after the Cupcake Battle finale tomorrow. Cee-cee and Max had crushed it yesterday and surely needed a day to rest, regroup, and prepare. But when her oldest sister had stopped by on her way home from the contest last night to share the big news in person, she'd walked in on Stephanie in tears after another brutal day with Pop.

As much as Stephanie had tried to convince her otherwise, Cee-cee had insisted on calling a three-sister meeting. She and Anna were due any minute. Just as Stephanie looked at her watch to confirm, there was a knock at the door followed by the sound of it opening.

"I'm here, and I brought wine," Anna called as she kicked off her boots at the doorway before padding into the living room in stockinged feet.

"Wow, you're looking better," Stephanie observed with a smile. She hadn't seen her younger sister in nearly a week, and what a difference those days had made. The bruising on her face was all but gone. More than that, it was like the fire was back, albeit a little less bright. Granted, she still looked tired, but the vitality that Anna always exuded was definitely on its way to returning, and Stephanie couldn't be happier.

"Thanks. I've been getting outside and doing more. I got some Christmas shopping done, and bought a tree that Max helped me decorate the other night. I'm in the holiday spirit for sure." Anna's smile faded and she looked uncharacteristically nervous. "I've also made a decision."

The conversation was interrupted by another knock and then Cee-cee's voice as she stepped into the house, closing the door with a bang.

"I brought wine...," she said, her boots banging to the floor before she made her way into the room, bottle aloft.

"Great minds," Anna said, holding up the same bottle of cheery, red Beaujolais nouveau.

Cee-cee laughed and then turned to Stephanie. "Love the tree, sis. So festive with all the golden garland!"

"Yeah, Pop thought so too. Reminded him of a strip club, apparently," she replied with a roll of her eyes. "You guys want to talk in the kitchen so we can open that?"

She sent a pointed glance to Pop's closed bedroom door and the others nodded, catching on quickly. His hearing wasn't great, and judging by the blare of the TV, he was knee-deep in *Matlock* reruns, so he wouldn't likely venture out of his room until dinnertime again, but the kitchen definitely offered more privacy.

"I know I already said this, but I'm so proud of you, Cee-cee. Who would've thought a year ago you'd be baking on a television show?" Stephanie marveled as she made her way around the kitchen, gathering wine glasses and an opener and meeting her sisters at the marble island.

"I can't wait until it airs and we can show all our friends!" Anna added, accepting the now-full glass Stephanie handed her.

"That's why I really hoped to avoid this discussion until after tomorrow. Seriously, I don't know what difference one more day will make..."

But Anna and Cee-cee both cut her short.

"It's not one day. It's been weeks, and if we could all pick the date and time that we'll reach the end of our rope, it would be a whole lot easier. But we can't. So let's rip this off fast, like a Band-Aid, shall we?" Cee-cee said, slipping into her big-sister role with the ease of a pro. "We need to decide what to do about Pop, and we need to do it today." She held up a hand. "I know, I know, change takes time and we might not be able to fix things overnight, but if we have a plan of action, at least you'll be able to see the light at the end of the tunnel. Who wants to go first?" Cee-cee looked around expectantly.

Stephanie took a sip of wine and then dove in.

"I went to Briar Cove a few days ago. Just to check it out," she assured them as they both looked at her, wide-eyed. "It was great. Like, so lovely. And then this thing happened."

She filled them in on all of it, the good, the bad, and the ugly. By the time she was done, both Anna and Cee-cee had tears in their eyes, same as Stephanie had the day she'd gone.

"I know that a nursing home is the right choice for a lot of people, and likely will be for Pop someday. But as much as he drives me batty, I'm just not ready yet."

"Me neither," Cee-cee admitted with a sad sigh, running a hand through her dark hair.

"Same," Anna said. "I know I haven't been around enough to really merit a full vote, but I've made some decisions, and from now on, I'm going to be. Maybe not twenty-four seven, three-sixty-five/seven, but I've already got some things in the works that, if they pan out, will allow me to travel a handful of times a year for a week at a time and still get to do what I love. You can count on me."

"Me too," Cee-cee said. "Once the contest is over, I'll have more time. I still want to expand the business, but I've already talked to Barb and she's very interested in more hours once the holidays are over. I'll have more time for Pop, for Max, and Gabe if he needs me. I needed the me time to really dig in and get the business started, but I also want balance. I want it all, and there's no reason I can't have it. It's just going to take some doing, but I'm ready to roll up my sleeves. So what do you need from us, Steph?"

A lump formed in Steph's throat. She was so full of gratitude for her sisters in that moment, she could barely speak. "I don't even know. I guess some time without Pop here. As much as I thought I hated an empty house when Paul was gone, I've come to value my time alone. If he could stay overnight somewhere a couple days a week, that would be great. I know that's tough with the apartments and—"

"What about a swap?" Anna asked, shrugging. "Once I'm cleared for lifting, I can come stay here, you go stay at my place. Kick back, sit on the couch and watch movies while you eat ice cream and revel in the silence."

"Same," Cee-cee said, eyes lighting up. "I can totally stay here when it's my night with Pop. Heck, you have that amazing Jacuzzi tub...let me at it!"

Stephanie considered that and realized that just the thought made her feel better.

"But that's not enough," Cee-cee said with a frown. "What about in-home nursing care a few days a week? At least in the interim until Eva comes back?"

"I'll come get him Monday, Wednesday, and Friday and take him to the senior center in the morning so you can just worry about getting ready for work—"

"And on those days, I'll pick him up from the senior center at five," Cee-cee finished for Anna, slapping a hand on the countertop. "We'll get a nurse for those evenings, so that gives you three full days to yourself. Then Anna and I can alternate weekends here. What do you say?"

Stephanie frowned. "Nurses like that are expensive, and I don't think his insurance covers—"

"I'll sell the lot."

Stephanie looked up with a start to find their father standing in the kitchen doorway, looking grim but determined.

"Pop…I don't know what you heard, but—"

"I came out to apologize, and heard you girls trying to figure out how to manage an ungrateful, cranky old man," he said with a sad smile. "And I want to help. I've been thinking about it awhile now…maybe that's why I've been so out of sorts. I wanted to rebuild the bungalow because it was a piece of your mother, but she's not going to be in it, is she? And the home we shared is gone. You three are my family now. You and my grandkids. If I can help out at the shop sometimes so I don't feel useless, and I can bark at those kids and help them keep their noses clean and teach them about life, that's enough of a purpose for me. I'll sell the lot as is, and we can use the money for my nurses and whosie-whatsits. Whatever I gotta do to make that not too hard on you girls is what I want to do."

The three of them stared at him in shocked silence, which Anna broke first.

"Who are you and what have you done with our father?" she demanded accusingly.

This earned her a hacking guffaw from the old man, and some of the aching tension drained from the room.

"I'm still the same son of a gun who raised you and drives you to drink, so don't get too excited," he grumbled, eyeing the half-empty bottle of wine. "I just realized I gotta start being a little nicer to people or nobody is going to want to come to my funeral when I'm dead. At least, that's what Eva told me, and I believe her. She gives it to me straight."

Stephanie made a mental note to thank Eva as she stood and approached her father and pulled him into a tight hug.

"I love you, Dad. We all do."

"I love you too, Stephanie. All three of you, more than life itself. Now let go of me," he said, wrestling away from her. "I gotta pee and my prostate ain't what it used to be."

Stephanie released him with a watery laugh and watched through blurry eyes as he left the room.

"Ooookay, then," Anna said softly. "So, that just happened."

"I think I need to sit down," Stephanie said, shaking her head, still bemused.

"I'm not going to fool myself into thinking he's turned over a new leaf. In fact, tomorrow he might not even remember he said it, but we were all witnesses and that's good enough for me. Let's contact a realtor first thing Monday morning and get the ball rolling," Cee-cee said decisively.

"Sounds like a plan," Anna agreed. "I know I can't do much right now, but I can definitely start making calls to get a nurse here ASAP, and now that I can drive, I'm free to take Pop to the senior center in the mornings."

"And I just need until Monday...one more day, Steph. Can you handle it?" Cee-cee asked, reaching for her hand and squeezing.

"You guys were right. I really do feel better already. I'm good. Now that we have a plan, I feel like a ten-ton weight is off my chest."

If only she could say the same about this whole Paul situation.

Another knock sounded at the door, and Cee-cee stood. "That will be Max. She asked if she could come by and have a glass of wine with us. Hope that's okay?"

"Of course," Stephanie said with a smile. She and her only niece hadn't gotten to spend a whole lot of time together since Max had been back in town, but she loved her dearly and was always happy to see her. When Cee-cee led her into the room a minute later, it was clear that the wedge between mother and daughter was gone, and they were both beaming.

"Hey Aunt Stephanie, Aunt Anna!"

"Congratulations, Team Burrows. You guys rock!" Anna said, rising to find another wine glass for Max.

"It's almost surreal," Stephanie marveled. "You should both be really proud."

The four women spent the next couple hours talking about everything under the sun. Cee-cee's nerves during the taping of the show, and her fears of losing along with her worries over the shop growing too fast if she won. Anna's dates with Beckett, and her decision to try to spend a lot more time in Bluebird Bay. Max's bookstore woes and potential solutions. They even talked about Stephanie's worries over Paul and her fruitless visit to Pietro's. Until this point, Max had always been like one of the kids, but she seemed so mature now. Including her rather than shielding her from the fact that all three of the elder women in the room had hopes and dreams and feelings felt natural...easy.

"So they didn't remember Uncle Paul at all at the restaurant?" Max asked softly.

"He wasn't a regular, and most of the staff has long since turned over since then. It was a total long shot," Steph admitted as she traced an errant drop of wine on the rim of her glass. "I know I need to let it go, but worry and doubt have sunk their little hooks into my brain. I just want to know if there was more to him…things I didn't know."

"I'd want to know too," Max admitted.

Cee-cee nodded, and Anna followed suit. "I know I told you it was nothing and you should forget it, but I understand. It's easier said than done. And while I stand by my initial statement—Paul loved you more than anything and wasn't doing anything shady—I think if you feel like you need to pursue this, you should. Whatever helps you sleep at night," Anna said with a grim nod.

"Speaking of sleeping, are you still having nightmares?" Stephanie asked, glad for their support but also ready to change the subject.

"The nightmares aren't going away," Anna admitted, draining her glass and setting it aside. "I've decided to talk to Doctor Epstein about my options at our next visit. I was in such a daze after I got the news, I wasn't in a place to listen carefully and ask questions. After attending a couple of the support group meetings, I think it's important for me to do that, and really dig into the risks versus the benefits of doing something more drastic to reduce my chances of the cancer returning. I'm a take-the-bull-by-the-horns person, and so far, I've let this diagnosis terrify me into being someone else. I need to face it and whatever it entails head-on so I can do what's right for me."

The others tipped their glasses in agreement, and all the while, Stephanie couldn't help but apply Anna's sentiments to her own situation as well. Was that what she'd been doing? Letting life, grief, and the past two years *happen* to her instead of leading the charge?

By the time her family took their leave, her mind was whirling like mad. Taking the bull by the horns meant actively trying to figure out what was going on with Paul before he died. Even though she knew there was a fair chance what she found could break her in two. But where would she even start?

As she flicked off the light beside her bed and snuggled deeper under the covers, she only knew one thing for sure. Whatever Paul was hiding, whatever it meant for the two of them and her rosy, cherished memories of their lives together...

She needed answers. And she needed them soon.

Chapter Twenty-Seven

We got this, Mom."

Cee-cee turned to face Max, returning her daughter's hand squeeze and realizing with a start that Max's free hand was locked with Mick's. The three amigos.

She glanced up at the balcony seating, scanning the expectant and excited faces of the spectators here to witness the finale. When she finally caught sight of Anna, who stood out in a bright red sweater as promised, Cee-cee let out a sigh. Anna, Steph, Gabe, and Sasha were seated side by side, and with Mick and Max in the trenches with her, she'd never felt so loved.

She'd tried to get more tickets, but each family was only given four, and Pop didn't want to miss his weekly poker game at the senior center anyway. Probably for the best. It would be a long day, and he'd have been miserable anyway.

The same could definitely not be said for the others, though. Her family was cheering and waving like loons, and a bubble of laughter escaped her lips.

"They're nuts," Max observed with a laugh.

"You guys are so lucky to have each other," Mick said with a warm smile. "The support feels great. Everyone believes in you, Cee-cee."

For second, the words paralyzed her as the pressure mounted. What if she failed? What if she lost and had to go home without the victory?

"Nothing," she murmured under her breath. Absolutely nothing. She'd leave here with her family, and they'd all go somewhere to eat and commiserate. And tomorrow, she'd wake up with a great guy, and great kids, and a business she loved. It was a pretty good deal.

The knowledge left her body warm and humming and her heart full. And when the host stepped up to the row of remaining bakers, she felt unstoppable.

There would be no playing it safe today. She was going to swing for the fences, and if she failed, so be it. She would fail after giving it her all.

They'd already been given their instructions and were standing on their marks when the cameras began to roll a moment later.

"Good morning, bakers!" the host said brightly. "Are we ready to find out our theme for the big finale?"

Cee-cee held her breath and squeezed her eyes closed as the crowd cheered around them.

Please be something I've planned for. Please be something I've planned for.

"We'd like each team to create a life-sized Christmas tree, complete with ornaments…"

Yesss. She and Mick had discussed some great ideas for Christmas tree structures that would knock their socks off!

"…and a partially edible lighting element. Obviously, not the lights themselves, but some decorative element needs to be. Think bold. Thing big. Think fifty-thousand dollars!" the host exclaimed with a wide grin.

Cee-cee's joy turned to terror. She hadn't even considered lights beyond grabbing a string of LEDs and draping them around the display.

Now what?

"Let's start with the basics, Mom. That way I can begin on the batters and get them in the ovens while you and Mick work out the design, okay?" Max patted her shoulder and gave her a reassuring smile. "It's all good. We just have to stay focused. Talk to me about flavors."

Grateful for the direction, Cee-cee closed her eyes and tried to think of what would make them stand out in this group of amazing bakers. For sure, Not Fudging Around would go for elegance and precision over joy and fun. She had a feeling the others might go that route as well.

"Let's go super bright and cheery. No elegant Victorian or silver and gold leaf on white, but more like a fantastical tree. Something that would make Wonka jealous. It's the perfect time for Mick's creamsicle cupcakes."

Wonka.

She snapped her fingers as another light bulb went off. "Candy is dandy but liquor is quicker! Our theme is Have Yourself a Boozy Little Christmas. We'll add a good dollop of orange liqueur to amp up the creamsicle icing. The recipe is in my notebook. Then, we'll do an eggnog cake with spiced whipped cream, and we'll make those sunny yellow. Next, we'll do a take on Anna's maple bacon pecan cupcakes by adding some bourbon. We'll use pink food coloring for those and top them with the ribbon candy I saw in the pantry. Last but not least, a hot chocolate, super fudgy cupcake topped with Irish cream infused homemade marshmallow topping. We'll dip them in colored white chocolate candy-melts to create a hard, shiny shell in cherry red and blue. It will be an explosion of color."

Max nodded excitedly. "I'll start on the batters we have recipes for. You work the display out with Mick," she said and then rushed to the pantry to gather ingredients.

Cee-cee found Mick staring down at her with a bemused smile.

"What?"

"You're gorgeous when you're thinking hard."

His words sent a bolt of sheer joy through her and the last of her nerves disappeared. They had a job to do, and they needed to get doing it.

"Come on, hit me with the ideas, boss," Mick urged as he hunkered over her sketch pad on the work table.

Ten minutes later, the two of them had laid out the whole concept.

A tree stand on the bottom, surrounded by piles of presents in colorful wrapping paper with matching bows. Then, a five-tier display painted green and filled with cupcakes ornaments. No tree just had a bunch of glass balls on it, so in between, Cee-cee planned to mix in some fun surprises made from rice cereal treats and covered in fondant. She was already picturing homemade-looking ornaments of gap-toothed children in school portraits, and a handful of snow globe ornaments made from blown sugar. The lighting element that had vexed her initially came to her as clear as day. A nest of spun sugar wrapped around a star tree topper that was covered in golden LED lights, like the North Star. It was a lot to tackle, but with Mick and Max by her side, she knew she could do it.

The next eight hours went by like a dream. In some ways, she never wanted it to end. She and Max in the kitchen, perfectly in sync like they'd been doing it for years.

Mick coming in and out with pieces of the display to show her or paint colors he wanted her approval on...looking up at the balcony and seeing the rest of her family there...watching her creation come to life before her eyes...it was all like nothing she'd ever experienced. She was doubly blessed to have loved ones she could count on and to have found her purpose for the second chapter of her life.

But the near-constant rush of adrenaline was draining, and by the time the buzzer sounded, she was shaking like a leaf.

It was only when she, Mick, and Max fell against one another in a sweaty group hug that she realized her whole body ached. Throbbing feet and back, which was one false move from spasming. She was a mess.

They'd done it, though, and as she disengaged from their hug, she caught sight of the finished product in its entirety for the first time.

"Wow."

Mick's single-word exclamation echoed her own thoughts.

She wanted to win—dang, she wanted to win bad—but no matter what...that? Was a work of art. An absolute celebration of her favorite holiday. If this was her one and only contribution to the baking world, she could die feeling proud of the accomplishment.

She paused and glanced around at the other displays, noting with surprise that one team hadn't finished in time. Their pulled sugar lighting element remained on their workstation, and their heads were hung in disappointment. Cee-cee wished she could run over and hug them. She glanced over at team Not Fudging Around and nodded as she realized this was the one to beat.

That was the one to beat. As she'd expected, they'd gone sleek and minimal—much more to her ex-husband's taste than her own—but it was sheer perfection. Nerves exploded in her belly as she wondered if her display was too childish next to theirs, but she shoved the worry aside.

It was done, and she wouldn't change a thing. She and Max had eaten themselves sick, trying each element and then each cupcake as a whole at every single stage of the game. Mick had nailed the display, and the decorations were on point and clean.

There was nothing now but for the judging.

***

"Amazing job, bakers!" the host said, shaking her head in wonder. "Truly magical. You should all be so pleased. Let's see what our judges think, shall we?"

She turned to face the judges, who were each dressed to the nines in holiday-themed formalwear.

The next twenty minutes crawled by at a snail's pace as they did their tasting. Their faces gave away nothing this time as they murmured to one another and cast furtive glances at various parts of each display. She wasn't sure, but she thought the mean judge might've cracked a smile when he leaned in to examine one of her portrait ornaments.

Once they had tasted all the different cupcakes, the host had the bakers line up. Cee-cee couldn't help but think it felt a little like a firing squad as she, Max, and Mick again clasped hands.

"This was one of the closest competitions we can remember," the mean judge said as he scanned their faces, his expression serious as a heart attack. "We had whimsy, sophistication, and beauty, along with a whole array of flavors. Our decision was not unanimous, but we all agree two teams stood out most. Step forward, Cee-cee's Cupcakes and Not Fudging Around."

Cee-cee's throat went bone-dry and they all stepped forward.

"Team Fudging, your display was breathtaking. Every detail was executed perfectly. Teem Cee-cee, what can we say? This was a celebration. We were grinning like fools watching you on the monitors when it all started to come together. They're both amazing displays, with totally different aesthetics, so we decided we couldn't judge on looks. Both were perfect tens on that front. We had to base our decision on flavor. And in that?" His gaze flicked from Team Cee-cee's Cupcakes to Not Fudging Around and then back again. "Team Cee-cee's Cupcakes edged out the win. Congratulations!"

The blood rushed to Cee-cee's head, and she heard nothing but the beat of her own heart.

They'd won.

They'd *won!*

Later, she would remember the praise of the other judges and teams as they crowded around her. She would recall the warmth of Mick's embrace and the sound of Max's screams of joy. But in that moment, it was all she could do to stay on her feet and keep herself from bursting into happy tears.

Her sister was cancer-free, her baby girl was safe, her man was by her side, and she'd just won the East Coast Holiday Cupcake Battle. Happy holidays, indeed.

Chapter Twenty-Eight

The residents of Bluebird Bay were so excited about Cee-cee's Cupcakes being in the competition, they set up a projection TV in the community center so the entire town could watch the finale together. It was hard for the Sullivan sisters because they were sworn to secrecy about the winner.

Anna had never been more proud of Cee-cee, not only because she won but because Cee-cee had balanced family and career and excelled at both. It was time for Anna to do the same.

No one was more surprised than Anna that she was ready for a career change that would let her spend most of her time in Bluebird Bay, but after her cancer scare and her blossoming relationship with Beckett, she was ready to settle down and form some roots. No, scratch that. She had roots. She was finally ready to let herself grow in the place she felt most loved.

At first she worried she'd let her cancer diagnosis make her decision for her—not because she'd realized what was important, but because it had made her timid and fearful of living her life. There was no doubt that Anna's diagnosis had caused her considerable anxiety, plaguing her with nightmares, but the diagnosis had made her realize she wanted to focus on the truly important things in her life—family...and a certain handsome brown-eyed man who made her toes curl.

They had hired a new temporary nurse for Pop, but since Eva's sister had gone to spend the holidays with her daughter in Manhattan, Eva had come back to town for the event and would be around through Christmas. She was in charge of Pop, who vacillated between pride that his daughter and granddaughter were going to be on TV and confusion as to why they were there.

Stephanie's kids had even come home early for Christmas, so everyone was truly together. Anna hoped it was less chaotic than Thanksgiving. So far, they were off to a good start.

Everyone had been eating cupcakes Cee-cee, Max, and Barb had baked for the viewing party, all in the flavors of the cupcakes they'd made on the show. With only a few minutes until airtime, the crowd of over one hundred people took their seats, then quieted when the show's theme music began to play. The crowd talked amongst themselves during commercials, but instantly hushed when the show came back on. Then when Cee-cee's Cupcakes was announced the winner, the room filled with deafening cheers of celebration, as though the town itself had won.

It occurred to Anna that home wasn't just her family but her community too. And to the town of Bluebird Bay, they were winners simply by association with one of their residents.

There were calls for Cee-cee to make a speech, and she was red-faced as she walked in front of the room, casting a pleading look to Max and Mick, who stood to the side.

"This is all you, Mom!" Max called out. "It's your night to shine!"

The people erupted again with cheers, some of them chanting Cee-cee's name. She stared out into the crowd teary-eyed as she kept saying "thank you."

Finally, everyone settled down, leaving a nervous-looking Cee-cee. She cleared her throat and said, "First of all, I wouldn't have even caught the eye of the producers of the competition if the citizens of Bluebird Bay hadn't given me their full support. You all helped put me on the map, so to speak."

The crowd erupted again.

When they settled down, Cee-cee continued, "I couldn't have done this without the support of my family. My sisters, Stephanie and Anna—you're the best sisters a woman could ever ask for. Also, to my father." She searched the crowd until she found him in the back of the room with Eva. "Thanks for eating all those cupcakes I made when we were kids. You always encouraged me to bake more." Ripples of laughter echoed through the room. "Thanks to my son Gabe and his fiancée Sasha, who offered me love, support, and encouragement when I said I was going to enter this crazy thing."

"I love you, Mom," Gabe called out.

"I love you too," she said, then blew him a kiss.

"But most of all, I want to thank my daughter Max and my boyfriend Mick. Max was my baking assistant, who took orders without question and believed in me even when I doubted myself."

"You had this, Mom!" Max yelled. "I knew it all along."

Cee-cee blew her a kiss too.

"And Mick..." Cee-cee's voice broke. "I wouldn't be nearly as successful as I am if this man hadn't believed in me since the first night I asked him to drop by the space and give me an estimate to get my cupcake shop up and running."

"It was the creamsicle cupcakes," he said with an ornery grin. "One taste and I was a goner."

Cee-cee grinned from ear to ear while the crowd laughed.

"And finally," she said, seeming to gain confidence with every word, "I want to say how proud I am of myself. When my husband asked me for a divorce, I had no idea what I was going to do. I was fifty-two years old and trying to figure out the second half of my life. I could have gotten stuck there, but I decided there was a whole lot more living to do, and I was grabbing the bull by the horns and living it." A huge smile spread across her face. "And now I'm the happiest I've ever been. So if you find yourself stuck—no matter how old or young you are—you can still find your way. It's never too late for a second act. Or third. Or however many it takes until you get it right." She gave them a little wave. "Thank you for coming out tonight. Now somebody better grab the rest of those cupcakes in the back because I'm not taking them home."

"Do you think that's true?" Maryanne Brown asked, moving closer to stand directly next to Anna.

Anna glanced around, sure she was talking to someone else, but it was just the two of them.

"Which part?" Anna asked.

"That it's never too late for a fresh start?"

Anna grinned. "I sure as heck hope so. I'm planning on one for myself." Then she pulled Maryanne into a hug. "It's time to let bygones be bygones, Maryanne." She released her and said, "Would you like to go out to lunch after the first of the new year?"

"Yeah," Maryanne said, looking shy. "I would."

"Good," Anna said. "We'll figure out when and where at the next meeting."

"Sounds good."

Beckett, who had been standing on Anna's other side, gave her a grin of approval.

The viewing party was a huge success, and after everyone left, the Sullivan sisters and their loved ones headed to the cupcake shop for a celebratory bottle of champagne… everyone except Pop. Eva had taken him home to bed.

Mick opened the bottle and poured glasses for everyone, and they waited for Cee-cee to speak.

"I want you all to know what I have planned for the prize money." She turned to Gabe and Sasha. "I'm giving you two half the money minus taxes for you to use on the wedding."

"Mom," Gabe protested, shaking his head. "You don't have to do that."

"I know," she said. "But I'm your mother and I want to." She turned to Max. "And the other half will go to Max and her bookstore. We'll make it the talk of the Maine coast."

"Mom," Max started to protest.

"Max, you just stop right there," Cee-cee said in a mock-serious tone. "It's my money and I can spend it how I see fit."

Tears streamed down Max's face. "Thank you."

Cee-cee nodded.

"To Cee-cee's Cupcakes!" Mick said, raising his glass.

"To Cee-cee's Cupcakes!" everyone else said in chorus.

They all took sips of their champagne, and Anna decided it was a good time to make her own announcement.

"I have something to tell you guys too," she said.

"We all know you're sticking around Bluebird Bay," Max said, beaming. "And other than Beckett Wright, I'm not sure anyone is more thrilled than I am."

To Anna's shock, she felt her face flush. "That's not what I was going to say." She took a moment to catch her breath, then said, "I've had several conversations with my doctors and a geneticist, and given Mom's history and my own genes, I'm scheduling a double mastectomy after I finish and heal from radiation."

The room was quiet before Cee-cee asked in a tight voice, "Did they find more cancer?"

"No," Anna said. "And this way, they likely won't. I have the gene that makes me likely to develop a different form of breast cancer, so I've decided to take preventive measures. I've given this a lot of thought, and since I made the decision, my anxiety has gotten much better. It's put my mind at ease."

Anna was under no delusions. She knew from talking to some of the women in her group that this surgery would be no walk in the park, and would likely have its own mental and physical ramifications. But she also knew this was the right decision for *her*, and that was all that mattered.

"We want what's best for you," Stephanie said. "And if that's what you need to do, we'll be here to help you through it all."

"Thank you," Anna said. "Truly." She glanced over at Beckett, wondering what he thought. It was early in their relationship, and this was a lot to spring on him. She probably should have told him in private.

He grabbed her hand and laced their fingers. "Whatever it takes to give you as many years as possible, because I plan to spend as many as I can with you."

Warmth spread through Anna's chest. "Thanks, Beckett."

Anna spent another twenty minutes with her family, then told Beckett she was ready to have him take her home.

As soon as they were in his truck, he said, "So you're planning to stick around, huh?"

"You caught that, huh?"

"Are you kidding me? I couldn't miss something like that," he said, grinning from ear to ear. "What helped you come to that decision?"

"Before you freak out and think I'm putting the cart before the horse, I'm not doing this because of you. It's just that I'm realizing what's important—family and people I love. I always knew my family was here waiting for me, but now I actually want to be here with them. So when I was offered a job as a photographer for a local preservation society, I jumped at the chance. And I'll still get to travel from time to time, but only a few times a year and for short stretches."

"That sounds great, Anna. The important thing is that *you're* happy."

"I am," she said. "And I will be. This is what I want."

Beckett pulled up in front of her apartment and put the car in park. "I wouldn't have freaked out," he said. "It's important you know that."

"What?" she asked, confused.

"If you'd made part of your decision because you didn't want to leave me—leave us—I wouldn't have freaked out." Then he leaned closer and kissed her.

She kissed him back, her heart filled with a contentment she had never known, and she knew she'd unintentionally told him a little white lie. Deep down, he'd been part of the reason she'd decided to stay. In the past, it would have filled her with panic. Now it filled her with peace. Anna might be a late bloomer, but she'd finally found home...and it had been in her backyard all along.

About the Author

Denise Grover Swank was born in Kansas City, Missouri and lived in the area until she was nineteen. Then she became nomadic, living in five cities, four states and ten houses over the course of ten years before she moved back to her roots. She speaks English and smattering of Spanish and Chinese which she learned through an intensive Nick Jr. immersion period. Her hobbies include witty Facebook comments (in own her mind) and dancing in her kitchen with her children. (Quite badly if you believe her offspring.) Hidden talents include the gift of justification and the ability to drink massive amounts of caffeine and still fall asleep within two minutes. Her lack of the sense of smell allows her to perform many unspeakable tasks. She has six children and hasn't lost her sanity. Or so she leads you to believe.

For more info go to: dgswank.com or denisegroverswank.com

Finding Home

About the Author

Christine Gael is the women's fiction writing alter-ego of USA Today Bestselling contemporary romance author, Christine Bell, and NYT Bestselling paranormal romance author, Chloe Cole.

Christine lives with her sweet, funny husband in South Florida, where she spends the majority of her day writing and consuming mass amounts of coffee. Her favorite pastimes include playing pickle ball and tennis year-round, and texting pictures of palm trees and the beach to her New England-based friends in the wintertime.

While Christine enjoys all types of writing but, at age 46, she's especially excited to be creating stories that will hopefully both entertain and empower the women in her own age group.

For more information visit her website at christinegael.com

24060352R00149